AGE of TIDES

National Bestselling Author

Myunique C. Green

Print Edition ISBN: 978-1-105-89605-7

Produced By iWriteBooks Publishing

MyuniqueGreen.com

OTHER BOOKS

Available in Digital & Paperback

Young Adult Fantasy
Everything That Glitters (Bloodlines Book 1)
Dead to Rights (Bloodlines Book 2)
Awakened (The Reignmere Chronicles Book 1)
Reaping 101

Sci-Fi & Dystopian
Cipher (Hybrid Horizons Book 1)
Talia (Hybrid Horizons Book 2)
Grand Rising
Zombies Anonymous
Heatfall

Literature & Fiction
Psinder
Hysteria
Professional Development
Linked By Ink (Available as Audiobook)
Hearts, Hype & Other Hoaxes

Women's Non-Fiction
The C is for Complex
To Mend a Broken Heart (Available as Audiobook)
Girl, It Hasn't Happened Yet!
Love Letters to Heaven

Mystery & Suspense
Chopped & Skrewed (Available as Audiobook)
Last Seen (Available as Audiobook)
Compulsive
Anywhere But Here
Miss America

PROLOGUE
The Pulse

Before there was light, there was movement.

The ocean existed first as breath—a slow inhale across an empty world, drawn from nothing and made into everything. It coiled, whispered, and gathered into weight, until the weight became water, and the water became memory.

From that memory came *Navedia.*

She was not born, not shaped—simply *realized,* a mind forming in the depths of unbroken sea. She sang the first current into being, and it answered her voice in spirals of sound and salt. Her song filled the void with warmth, and life unfolded like light caught beneath glass.

The coral came next, soft as thought. Then the reefs, the kelp, the great leviathans that swam through the dark with lantern eyes. And in time, the sea learned to speak—not in words, but in rhythm. Every tide, every wave, every ripple against stone whispered the same message: *I am alive.*

But creation, as always, grew restless.

Navedia watched her world bloom and shift, and she loved it too fiercely. Her pulse spread through the deep, binding everything to her will—the current obeyed, the coral bent, and the water thickened with her command. Harmony, she believed, could exist only in sameness. And so she sang louder, shaping everything in her image.

It was beautiful. It was endless. It was wrong.

For even in the deepest sea, there is hunger for difference.

The coral, alive with her voice, began to change on its own. It grew in colors Navedia had not sung, formed patterns her rhythm could not hold. And in that change was defiance. Life had found a way to move without her song.

Furious, Navedia poured her essence into the depths to reclaim what was hers. But her pulse—too vast, too powerful—fractured. The sea convulsed. The Heartwake, the place where her voice had first touched creation, became a wound that burned with eternal light.

Her followers, those first merfolk born from her tide, tried to mend it. They called upon gods older than her name and sealed the Pulse inside a cage of coral and current. They made a covenant: *the sea would flow one way, and its power would belong to none.*

They built cities upon the wound. They crowned kings. They wrote laws in salt and scripture, pretending not to feel her hum beneath the floor of their temples.

But the Heartwake never stopped breathing.

Through centuries of silence, it pulsed—soft, steady, patient. It waited for one who could carry both song and silence. One who could bridge the stillness above and the depth below.

When the time came, she was born not from coral or tide, but from *love*. A daughter of two worlds. A girl with a Spark in her heart and the sea in her veins.

Her name was *Maren*.

And when she took her first breath, the ocean shivered—for the Pulse had found its echo once more.

CHAPTER ONE

The Scales

The water always feels different on mornings like this—thicker somehow, syrupy with nerves and shimmer. Even the currents seem to hold their breath, waiting for the song to start.

From the palace balcony, I can see the whole of Lurea unfurling beneath me: ribbons of coral towers, each crowned with lanterns that sway with the tide. The city hums—not sound exactly, but movement. Schools of silverfish streak between pearl archways, guild banners flutter in the filtered light, and the sea itself glows with the kind of radiance that makes you forget the world above even exists.

Today is the Pulse Rite. Not mine, of course.

The thought still pricks like sea glass.

Every noble child is tested before the coral ring—except me. My father says it's out of respect for the throne. Everyone else says it's because the sea already refused me.

But I'm not staying hidden in the palace again. Not this time.

I slip through the hall's kelp curtains before dawn, the palace guards half asleep at their posts. My scales catch the faintest bit of the morning light—opaline, almost translucent—and I curse them under my breath. There's no disguising royal skin, no matter how quietly you swim.

The city opens beneath me, alive and breathing. The currentways spiral down like veins of light, ferrying early traders toward the Plaza of Flow. I catch the edge of one and let it carry me, the rush pushing against my cheeks. Salt bites sweetly on my tongue. The water thrums in my ears. For a few seconds, I almost forget why I'm here.

Then the plaza rises ahead, crowded with hundreds of onlookers—Flowed families with gleaming seals on their arms, guild elders draped in kelp finery, soldiers hovering like anchored shadows. At the center of it all floats the coral ring: a living circle pulsing faintly pink and gold. The Rite.

I stay near the edge, hidden among streamborn children too young to recognize me. Their laughter bubbles through the water, bright and soft.

The coral masters begin their chant, each voice woven with the next. A low thrumming builds—felt more than heard. The sea stirs in answer, and the first initiate swims forward. A boy from the Pressure Guild family, his chest puffed with certainty. He places his palms on the coral and closes his eyes.

Light blooms.

It races up the spires like veins igniting, turns the water around him molten gold. The crowd gasps in delight. "Pressure current," someone whispers. "Strong."

He grins as the guild sigil brands faintly across his wrist, shimmering with pride.

One by one, they step into the ring: Bloom, Tide, Light, Shadow. The coral answers each with a different hue, painting the plaza in rippling color. Each success earns applause that sounds like rainfall, echoing softly against the domes.

And then there's silence.

Because she's next—the last girl of the day. Younger than me by two years, but born into everything I'm not. The daughter of a councilor, her scales polished to pearl, her smile poised.

When she steps into the ring, the coral glows immediately. Not with one color, but several, cascading like sunrise through the reef. Even the sea itself seems to lean closer.

It's too much beauty at once. I can't help it—I drift forward, caught by it like a fish in a net.

The guards part the crowd for her family, their seals gleaming red and white. And I see my father among them, at the dais. King Thalen. Calm, solemn, watching the ceremony as if every light affirms his order.

He doesn't see me yet.

My pulse quickens. The water around me stirs—not the sea's doing, but mine. It always does when I'm anxious, like it can't decide if it wants to follow or flee.

Before I know it, I've crossed half the plaza.

Someone murmurs, “Is that—?”

I reach the ring just as the coral’s light fades from the other girl’s hands. My fingers hover over the surface. It’s alive, I can feel it—warm, faintly vibrating. It should respond. Everything in this world responds to the Flow.

Except me.

“Princess Maren,” one of the elders says sharply. “You are not—”

I touch the coral.

At first, nothing. Then—silver. Not the gold of Tide, not the green of Bloom, but a cold, bright silver that flashes through the ring like lightning through glass.

The glow lasts one heartbeat before dying entirely.

The water goes still. The chanting stops. Even the lanternfish hovering above freeze, their lights dimming.

I hear the whispers before I see the faces.

“Drainblood.”

“Stillborn Tide.”

“Navedia’s curse.”

The words slide through the crowd like oil. My throat tightens. The coral, still beneath my hand, feels like stone now.

And then my father’s voice cuts through the silence. “Enough.”

The word carries weight—every current bends slightly toward it. The crowd falls quiet. He looks at me across the plaza, his expression unreadable behind the refracted light.

"Return to the palace."

There's no anger in his tone, which is worse. Anger means feeling. This is... order.

"Yes, Father." My voice comes out thinner than I'd like.

I back away from the ring, every eye following. The coral remains dark, lifeless. For the first time in my life, I wish the sea itself would swallow me whole.

The silence breaks not with words, but with movement—hundreds of tails shifting, scales flashing in the dim light. It sounds like rainfall against glass, a thousand small escapes as everyone pretends not to stare. The crowd bends around me like a current flowing past a rock too stubborn to move.

A pair of courtiers murmur prayers into the water. The syllables curl like ink, rising until they dissolve. The girl who passed the Rite clings to her mother's arm, her new guild mark gleaming bright as sunrise. I catch her looking at me—pity soft and sharp all at once—and that's somehow worse than mockery.

My father's attendants are already closing ranks, their coral staffs glowing faintly as they usher him from the dais. He doesn't look back. He doesn't have to. I can feel the weight of his disappointment press against my chest harder than the ocean ever could.

The air—or whatever passes for it down here—grows heavy. I try to breathe, but the water tastes bitter, metallic, like it's rejecting me too. I turn away before anyone can see the tremor in my hands.

A guard steps forward as if to escort me, but the look I give him stops him cold. I may be useless to the sea, but I'm still a princess. The title has to count for something.

I swim toward the outer gates, head bowed, each motion careful and deliberate. The coral path beneath me flickers, unsteady, as though my shadow dims its light. My reflection ghosts across the glass walls—eyes too human, scales too dull.

Around me, the ceremony resets. Servants clear away offerings, guild banners fold in on themselves, laughter returns like nothing ever happened. The sea moves on. It always does.

I want to scream, to send every current crashing into the plaza until they can't ignore me anymore. But when I open my mouth, no sound comes out—just a stream of bubbles that rise uselessly toward the ceiling of light.

So, I let the tide take me.

It pulls at my hair, at the fabric of my ceremonial wrap, tugging me backward through the coral arches. The farther I swim, the more distant the music becomes—flutes and shells and hollow drums fading until all I hear is the beat of my own pulse.

The palace lights gleam faintly on the horizon, their gold haze threading through the water like distant fire. The whole city still glows—its spires like giant candles, its streets laced with flowing light—but none of it feels warm.

I swim aimlessly, letting the current drag me through the city's lower channels. The market shells are closing; streamborn vendors gather their glowing wares, the scent of brinefruit and crushed kelp hanging heavy in the water.

Two children dart past, laughing, their small currents leaving glittering trails behind them. I press my palm to my chest, feeling nothing but the faint beat of my own heart.

I should go home. Pretend to be obedient. But the thought of gliding through those palace doors—of facing my father's silence and my mother's pity—makes my stomach knot.

Instead, I drift upward, toward the Light Veil.

The water grows brighter the higher I swim, shot through with sunbeams that look solid enough to touch. No one is allowed near the surface; it's considered sacred, dangerous, both. But it's the only place that feels mine.

When I reach the ridge, I pause and look down at Lurea. From here, the kingdom looks perfect—rings of coral blooming outward from the palace, currentways weaving between them like silver threads. If I squint, I can almost believe I belong to it.

Then a flicker catches my eye—something far below.

A single blue light, faint and pulsing from the trench's direction.

The Drains' color. The one we're told to fear.

It winks once, twice, as if in greeting.

And for the strangest moment, I feel the water move around me—not in a push, not in a flow, but a pulse that starts at my ribs and spreads outward.

I press my hand against my sternum. There's a tiny snap, like air escaping. The water tingles.

Then it's gone.

The pulse fades as quickly as it came, leaving only a tremor in the water and the echo of my heartbeat ricocheting in my ribs. I stay there for a while, suspended between currents, afraid that if I move, whatever that was will vanish completely—or worse, come back stronger. The sea feels too close, too aware, like it's watching from every direction at once.

Tiny plankton drift through the glow, brushing my skin like the touch of minnows. When I exhale, the bubbles rise in uneven bursts, carrying the taste of salt and metal. It feels like breathing after lightning. My hands still tingle. I stare at them until the last flicker of silver fades from my fingertips, until I can almost convince myself it never happened.

Below, the city hums on. Coral towers pulse with warm light, and the highways of current wind lazily through them, ribbons of pale gold that pay me no mind. A shoal of jellyfish passes, their bells rising like lanterns toward the upper reefs. The world moves the way it always has, steady and sure, as if I didn't just see it hesitate.

I look once more toward the trench. The blue light is gone now, swallowed by distance. Only darkness remains—thick, endless, familiar. The kind that feels like silence pressed against the skin.

When I finally turn away, my reflection wavers in the glassy reef wall beside me: eyes wide, hair caught in a slow current, the faint outline of a girl trying to disappear. For a heartbeat, I almost do. The pull of the deep tugs at me, gentle and constant, whispering promises I can't quite hear.

I force myself to swim upward. The current resists, reluctant to let go. Each stroke feels heavier than it should, like the water itself is testing my resolve. By the time I breach the outer rim of the plaza, my chest aches from the effort.

The lights of Lurea stretch before me again—familiar, brilliant, impossibly far away. I follow the current home, moving through corridors of coral and glass, past gardens asleep in their own glow. The excitement of the Rite is long gone; only the faint residue of celebration lingers, a distant vibration in the water.

By the time I return to the palace, the hallways are empty. Only the glow of kelp lanterns guides the way, their light shifting from gold to green with the passing of the hour.

I pause before the great doors of the throne hall. Beyond them, my father will be conferring with the Depth Council about what I've done—about what the coral did, or didn't do.

I almost turn away.

But the door opens first.

He stands at the far end of the chamber, a silhouette framed by the Crown Wave—a living arc of suspended water that ripples with every word he speaks. The throne itself glows faintly beneath it, veins of silver current spiraling through the coral seat.

"Close the door," he says without looking at me.

I obey.

"Do you know what that was, today?" His voice is calm. Too calm.

"I wanted to see the Rite."

"You disobeyed an order."

"Yes."

"And humiliated the royal line."

I flinch, then catch myself. "I didn't mean—"

“The coral died, Maren.” His gaze cuts through the dim light. “The sea recoiled. Do you understand what that means?”

“It—maybe it was a mistake. Maybe—”

“There are no mistakes in the Pulse.” He sighs, a sound like shifting currents. “Your mother’s experiments have filled your head with impossible ideas. You are of the sea, but not of its will. Accept that.”

I bite back the words that rise—sharp, defensive, useless. The silence between us stretches. The Crown Wave above his head ripples faintly, reacting to the tension neither of us will name.

When he finally speaks again, it’s quieter. “Stay out of sight until the Drift Festival. I’ll have no more omens attached to this family.”

He turns away before I can answer.

I leave the hall before he can see the water trembling around my hands.

The corridor beyond is colder, the kind of chill that seeps into your chest and won’t leave. My reflection ripples in the marble coral walls—distorted, doubled, half of me light, half shadow. Guards posted along the archways bow as I pass, their eyes fixed straight ahead, pretending not to notice the faint disturbance trailing in my wake. The water around me stirs wrong, too fast, as if it’s nervous.

I swim without aim, through halls carved with the kingdom’s history—murals of past rulers commanding the tides, the gods blessing their reigns with radiant currents. Every figure glows with the Pulse, their hands outstretched in harmony with the sea. Not one of them looks like me.

At the end of the hall, I pause before the statue of Marelis, goddess of Bloom. Her coral vines twist upward, each one tipped with pearlescent light that sways gently with the motion of the water. I touch her foot, hoping for warmth, for even a spark of acknowledgment. The coral beneath my fingers stays cool and still.

A bubble slips from my throat, small and shaky. I don't bother chasing it as it rises.

Servants cross the corridors ahead, carrying trays of luminous shells from the feast hall. They lower their voices when they see me, their words dissolving into polite silence. I drift past them, nodding once. One drops her gaze; the other pretends to adjust the lantern in her hands. The moment stretches thin, then breaks, leaving only the echo of my passing.

The palace gardens open before me, vast domes of glass and coral, each archway glowing with slow, rhythmic light. I push through them in silence. Kelp trees sway overhead, brushing the tops of my shoulders like sighs. The scent of brinefruit and crushed shells lingers, remnants of the ceremony feast that ended hours ago.

In the center pool, the palace's heart coral hums faintly, its glow steady, content. I envy it for knowing its purpose.

The ache behind my ribs grows sharper, a pulse that doesn't match the sea's. I curl my fists until my nails dig against my palms. A flash of static jumps between my fingers—tiny, invisible, gone before I can be sure it was real. The garden lights flicker once, as though startled.

I exhale and press forward through the last corridor, up the spiraling passage that leads to my quarters. The ascent is slow; the water thickens with each turn, heavy with quiet. When I reach the upper wing, the palace feels deserted—no laughter from the servants' quarters, no echo of council arguments from below. Just silence and the soft hum of the kelp lanterns that line the walls.

The door to my chamber slides open with a sigh. I step inside, feeling the pressure of the outside world slip away like a weight unclasped from my shoulders.

Later, in my room, I float near the ceiling and stare through the glass dome that serves as a window. Outside, lantern rays drift past—massive, translucent creatures that carry the soft light of the upper sea.

They remind me of my little sister, Saphra, and her habit of chasing them through the palace gardens. I used to follow, pretending to catch her just before she wandered into forbidden currents. Back then, she'd call me brave.

Now she doesn't call me anything at all.

The thought stings more than I expect.

I close my eyes and try to breathe. The water presses cool against my skin, soothing, constant. But underneath that calm is something else—an ache that feels too alive to ignore.

I lift my hand and watch small air bubbles escape my fingertips. They rise a few inches, then flatten into silver static before dissolving.

Static.

That's what the coral looked like when I touched it. Not light, not current—something sharper. Something that didn't belong.

"Drainblood," the crowd had whispered. "Stillborn Tide."

Maybe they're right.

But the memory of that blue flicker from the trench won't leave me. It felt like it saw me. Like it was waiting.

I wonder if the Drains ever feel this kind of pull—this restlessness that hums beneath the bones, whispering that the world isn't as finished as everyone insists.

I think about the way the coral glowed silver before it died, and I don't feel entirely ashamed. Just... curious.

The thought keeps circling, soft as a current, impossible to hold still. What if it hadn't died at all? What if it had only changed—shifted into something the sea didn't yet understand? The idea feels dangerous and delicious, like leaning too far over a drop just to see how deep it goes.

I press my palm against the wall beside my bed. The coral there is smooth, warm from the palace's inner flow. When I concentrate, I almost imagine a rhythm under the surface, faint but steady, answering me. But when I blink, it's gone. Maybe it was never there.

The lantern rays drift closer to the window, their bodies pulsing in lazy synchronization, casting long waves of light across my ceiling. The room becomes an imitation of the open sea—blue and white ripples sliding over my skin, across the shelves, through my hair. I watch them until the ache in my chest quiets to a murmur.

Still, sleep doesn't come. Every time I close my eyes, I see that flash again—the silver light, sharp and cold, cutting through the coral ring. The moment before everything went dark. It doesn't feel like failure anymore. It feels like a beginning that everyone else mistook for an ending.

I turn over, restless, the sheets whispering against my scales. The hours stretch thin, marked only by the slow color shift of the lantern outside my door—from amber to green, from green to the palest blue. The palace breathes around me, alive and unaware.

When the last trace of gold drains from the hall and the world falls into that soft, weightless hush that only exists between tides, I finally give up on pretending. I swing my legs from the bed, careful not to stir the water too loudly. The chill feels clean against my skin, almost welcoming.

The palace is quiet when I leave again, hours past midnight. I slip through the gardens—corridors of coral that glow faintly green, their tendrils brushing my arms like nervous hands.

There's a spot I go when I can't sleep: a hollow between two ridges where the palace light doesn't reach. From there, you can see the Trench Below as a ribbon of blue fire stretching into forever.

Tonight it feels closer than usual.

I settle on the ridge, knees pulled to my chest, and watch the faint shimmer far beneath. The sea murmurs softly, the kind of sound that lives between thought and dream.

I talk to it sometimes, half expecting it to answer.

"I didn't mean to break your ceremony," I whisper into the dark. My voice comes out as a series of bubbles that drift upward, tiny and bright. “But you have to admit—it was a little funny.”

A lone jelly drifts past, trailing threads of gold. I grin despite myself. “See? You get it.”

The levity fades when I glance down again. That same blue pulse flickers once more, deep in the trench. I should be afraid. Everyone says the Drains are cursed, that their light is the ocean’s sickness.

But something about it feels... alive.

The water around me stirs faintly, tugging at my hair. A current, small but deliberate, brushes my shoulder like a whisper.

Then, faintly, I feel it—a pulse beneath my skin, answering. The first beat of something that shouldn’t exist. It’s gone before I can be sure it was ever there. Still, I smile. Because for once, the sea moved when I did.

CHAPTER TWO

The Queen

Mother's laboratory always hums. Not musically, not pleasantly—more like the sea itself trying to whisper secrets through the walls.

I push open the coral door, and the sound sharpens into something alive. Rows of glass flasks line the shelves, their contents glowing in pulses that don't match one another. Coral roots twist through the walls like veins, their tips capped with metal rings that spark faintly when touched by the water's flow. Everything smells faintly of salt and copper—clean and wrong at the same time.

Mother stands at the center table, her hair bound with a silver filament, the loose strands drifting in delicate waves around her face. She's humming softly, though I can't tell if it's a tune or just concentration. Her hands move quickly, rearranging instruments that shimmer with their own light.

"You shouldn't sneak up on people who work with volatile elements," she says without turning.

"I didn't sneak," I answer. "You just don't listen when you're obsessed."

That earns a small smile. "A fair point. Come here, then. Let me look at you."

I swim closer, trying not to disturb the suspended scrolls of kelp parchment that hang around the room. The ink written there glows blue—notes, formulas, sketches of things the Council would call heresy.

She studies me the way others study maps—searching for something hidden in the lines. "You've been out again."

"Only to the gardens."

"And before that?"

"To the ceremony."

Her hands still. "I told you not to."

"I know."

Her gaze lifts to mine, all softness gone. "They don't understand you, Maren. They don't want to. Every time you put yourself in front of them, you give them another reason to call you cursed."

"I didn't do anything," I whisper.

"The coral says otherwise."

The silence between us thickens. The sea outside the lab seems to hold its breath. I look past her, to the main table—its surface a chaos of tools, crushed shells, shards of glowing crystal. In the center sits a small sphere of blue glass, pulsing faintly like a heartbeat.

"Is that Heartwake?" I ask.

Her expression softens just enough to let pride through. "A purified fragment. Veyne's people smuggled it up before the Trench closed again. It's stable enough for testing—if handled correctly."

"You're not supposed to have that."

She laughs quietly. "Half of what I'm not supposed to have keeps this kingdom alive."

The glow from the Heartwake sphere casts her skin in rippling light. Beneath her collarbones, faint veins of coral glimmer under the surface—a lattice of living pink lines that shift as she breathes.

"Does it hurt?" I ask, nodding toward them.

"Sometimes." She presses a hand to her chest. "But pain is how we know we're changing."

She gestures to a seat beside the table. "Come. I need a sample."

I hesitate. The last time she said that, I spent three days with my arm bandaged and the strange buzzing in my veins.

"What are you testing now?"

"Compatibility. You and the Heartwake share a frequency—one that defies the sea's order. I think I can prove it's not corruption but adaptation."

"That sounds exactly like something the Council would call corruption."

"Then I simply won't tell them."

Her tone is light, but her eyes are fierce. When she moves, the coral in her lungs glows brighter, pulsing in rhythm with her heart. It's mesmerizing—terrifyingly beautiful.

I extend my arm. “Fine. Make it quick.”

She takes a slender needle of bone and glass, sliding it into a vial of glowing solution before pressing it gently against my skin. The sting is brief. A ribbon of red swirls into the vial, mixing with the luminous blue.

The liquid reacts instantly—flaring bright, then dimming, then sparking again, tiny filaments of light snapping through it like lightning in miniature. The glow spreads up the glass, crawling toward her fingers.

“Mother?”

She’s watching too intently to hear me. The reflection of the light dances across her face, illuminating every line of exhaustion, every scar. Then the vial trembles violently in her hand.

“Selara!”

The glass fractures with a sharp crack. Blue veins of light spill outward, snapping through the water. The entire lab flickers; the coral walls convulse as though struck. I lurch backward, shielding my eyes. The shock is brief but strong enough to make the instruments clatter from their perches.

When the light finally fades, Mother is holding the remains of the vial, her expression unreadable. Tiny shards drift around her like dust. The fluid is gone—absorbed, dissolved, maybe consumed.

Her hand is trembling.

“Did it hurt you?” I ask.

“No,” she says too quickly. Then softer: “No. It just... reacted.”

“With what?”

She doesn't answer. She gathers the fragments carefully, tucking them into a sealed container, then wipes the table clean with mechanical precision. Every movement is deliberate, hiding the evidence before I can ask more.

"Promise me you won't tell your father," she says.

"He'll ask about the power flicker."

"Then say it was a surge in the Flow chamber. Say anything else."

"Why hide it? If you found something—"

"Because discovery doesn't mean safety." Her tone sharpens. "The Council would call it proof of impurity. Your father would see it as confirmation of the curse. Either way, you'd be locked away before I could finish what I've started."

I stare at her, the flickering light from the Heartwake sphere painting her features in alternating shades of devotion and dread.

"What have you started?"

Her lips curve faintly, almost a smile, almost a wound. "A future where you won't have to apologize for existing."

The silence that follows feels holy. I don't trust myself to speak.

Finally, she turns away, her voice suddenly tired. "Go, Maren. Rest. I need to... recalibrate."

I swim toward the door, glancing back once. The glow beneath her skin flickers erratically now, brighter than before, like something inside her is listening to something I can't hear.

When the door seals behind me, the corridor feels colder.

As I drift back toward my chambers, I press my hand to my chest where she drew the blood. Beneath my skin, something faintly sparks—too small to see, too real to ignore.

I keep swimming. I don't look back.

The corridors stretch endlessly, the water thick with silence. My pulse feels off-tempo with the sea again—too quick, too human. I press harder against my chest, willing it to calm, to sync, but the spark lingers beneath my skin like a secret refusing to sleep.

By the time I reach the family wing, the palace lights have dimmed to their late-evening hue—a deep, steady gold that pools in corners like candlelight. I expect the halls to be empty, but soft laughter echoes from the nursery dome.

Saphra.

Her voice always sounds like sunlight filtered through water—warm, bright, impossible to stay angry near.

I hover outside the archway, watching her through the thin veil of coral beads that hang as a curtain. She's floating upside down above her bed, arms outstretched, her hair fanned around her like a halo of spun glass. The Veil Ray—her pet manta—circles lazily above her head, trailing glimmering ribbons of light.

When she spots me, she squeals. "Maren! You're home!"

She flips upright and swims straight into me, nearly knocking me back into the hall. Her arms wrap around my middle, tiny but fierce. The contact startles the spark in me—it flares, faint but real, a quick pulse beneath my skin.

"Careful," I say softly, but I don't push her away.

She leans back, eyes wide. "You smell like the lab again."

I laugh once, short and quiet. "Do I?"

"It's that metal taste in the water. Mother's been in there too long." Her nose wrinkles. "She forgets to eat when she's working. I brought her coral biscuits but she said she'd 'recalibrate' them later. What does that even mean?"

"It means she's trying to fix things that don't need fixing."

Saphra tilts her head, studying me the way she studies her glowing garden in the mornings. "Like you?"

I falter. "Maybe."

She bites her lip, then floats backward, the Veil Ray following like a loyal shadow. "Zeke says people are scared because they don't understand you. I think they're just boring."

A laugh escapes me before I can stop it, small and unsteady. "You think so?"

"I know so." She crosses her arms, frowning like a miniature queen. "If I had your stillness, I'd sit in the middle of the market and not move at all. Just to see what happens."

"They'd whisper," I murmur.

"They already whisper," she says simply. "But they whisper about everyone. The trick is to make them whisper something beautiful."

Her words hang between us, too wise for her age. The spark in my chest flickers again—warmer this time.

I reach out and brush a strand of hair from her forehead. “You’re going to rule the sea one day, you know that?”

She grins. “Only if you teach me how to break it first.”

I shake my head, smiling despite the ache building behind my ribs. “Don’t ever change, Saphra.”

“I won’t,” she says with the stubborn certainty only a child can carry.

We stay like that for a while, the two of us suspended in the dim glow of her room. The Veil Ray drifts between us, its translucent wings brushing against my arm, leaving trails of light that fade as quickly as they appear.

When she finally yawns, I tuck her into the bed of woven kelp. She curls into it like a pearl inside a shell, the glow from her manta spreading a soft halo over her.

“Goodnight, sparkless sister,” she says, half teasing.

“Goodnight, little bloom.”

As I turn to leave, the Veil Ray glides after me to the doorway, pausing there as if reluctant to let me go. Its glow flutters once, twice, before dimming to match the lanterns in the hall.

I glance down at my hands again. The faintest trace of light answers from beneath my skin, so soft I might’ve imagined it.

For Saphra’s sake, I pretend I don’t see it.

CHAPTER THREE

The Others

Training mornings begin with light and noise. The palace courtyard fills with bodies in motion, each strike of a blade or sweep of a current echoing through the water like a heartbeat. The coral pillars surrounding the arena shift with the tide, glowing faintly to mark each student's pulse.

I arrive late, still tasting copper from last night's sparks. Zeke and Saphra are already center ring with the others—circling, weaving, perfect little heirs of the sea. Their scales catch the filtered sunlight, scattering it in gold and green flashes.

"Princess of Still Water," Neris calls when she notices me. Her smile is polished, her tone sugar over stone. "Didn't think you'd show."

Tarek's head lifts at once. "She's cleared to train like everyone else."

"That's generous," Neris says, drawing a lazy spiral in the sand with her trident tip. "The coral still hasn't forgiven her."

Damon glances up from his corner, dark eyes steady. He says nothing, but the look he gives her makes her flinch.

I ignore them and take my position. The water here feels different—denser, weighted by so many strong currents colliding. Every breath is work. Every movement leaves a faint shimmer of silt in my wake.

Zeke swims forward, his jaw tight. "Ready?"

"As I'll ever be."

He strikes first, the pressure around him tightening until the water itself sharpens. It's like fighting inside a heartbeat, the space between us compressing with every shift of his blade. I twist away, slower than I should be, my hair fanning into his path. His next move pulls the current wrong, a whip of force that slams into my shoulder.

Pain explodes through me. The water tilts. I hit the sand hard enough to see stars scatter through the murk.

Zeke's expression cracks. "Maren—"

"I'm fine." My voice sounds like it belongs to someone else. I push to my feet, ignoring the sting. The ache blooms down my arm, bright and immediate. The court trainers murmur from their observation perch, too quiet to hear but loud enough to understand.

Neris drifts closer, pity twisting her smile. "Pressure and stillness don't mix. The sea decides who belongs, Maren. Maybe it's time you stopped arguing with it."

Before I can answer, Tarek moves between us. His shadow blocks her glow, solid and unmoving. "Maybe the sea's waiting for someone who doesn't listen to it."

Neris laughs, soft and brittle. "That's not how it works."

"Maybe not for you."

The water cools around them, the kind of quiet that comes before a storm. Damon drifts nearer, his robes trailing like ink in the current. "The sea has more than one will," he says, voice low enough that only I hear.

Something in me steadies at that.

Zeke turns to the trainers, his posture sharp again, all guilt tucked behind duty. "She's finished for the day," he says.

"I said I'm fine," I repeat, but my shoulder throbs where his current struck. Tiny sparks of pain travel down my arm, too familiar to ignore. I can feel the water around me resist, as if the sea itself recoils from the contact.

The others resume drills, their movements precise and effortless. I watch them glide through patterns I've memorized but never mastered, every strike an act of belonging. My reflection ripples in the arena floor, fractured by the flow.

When the session ends, the heirs disperse in bursts of color—Bloom greens, Tide silvers, Pressure golds. I linger at the edge until the water clears, the arena settling back into stillness.

Tarek waits for me near the gate, arms folded, expression somewhere between concern and quiet fury. "You should've told him to hold back."

"He didn't mean to."

"Intent doesn't fix a bruise."

I flex my arm, wincing. "It's not just a bruise."

He studies me for a long moment, then nods toward the far coral steps leading to the gardens. "Walk with me. You need to let the current shift before you tear it open again."

I follow him. The path winds through low coral arches, the water here clearer, calmer. The noise of training fades until only the soft rustle of kelp remains.

When we reach the overlook, I stop and let the silence settle. Below us, the city of Lurea stretches wide and radiant, its towers breathing light into the ocean's dark.

Tarek leans on the railing, studying me. "They don't see what I see."

"What do you see?"

"Someone the sea's trying to figure out. Give it time."

"Time's what gets people exiled," I say quietly.

He looks away, and for a while neither of us speaks. The current shifts, gentle and cool, brushing over my skin like a question. My shoulder aches, but the pain feels distant now—like the aftertaste of lightning.

I close my eyes, breathe, and for one fleeting moment, I swear the sea breathes with me.

The current brushing past my skin feels faintly alive—curious, as if testing what kind of creature I am.

"I don't think it knows what to do with me," I say at last. "I'm supposed to flow, but I can't. I don't even know what that feels like."

Tarek doesn't answer right away. He pulls a stray kelp strand from his hair, wrapping it tight around his finger until it splits. "The Flowed say the Pulse speaks to them," he says finally. "They describe it like a song in their veins. I've never heard it, either. Maybe we're deaf in different ways."

"That's comforting," I say, smiling faintly.

He grins back. "You're welcome."

The smile fades from my face as I look out over the city. From here, Lurea is breathtaking. Bioluminescent canals twist between coral towers, each lit by the guild colors—gold for Pressure, green for Bloom, violet for Tide. In the distance, the Palace of Flow glows like a pearl cradled in living stone. But beneath all that beauty is something older: the ocean's pulse. I can't hear it, but I can feel the vibration, deep and far below, like a giant creature sleeping under the reef.

"Do you ever wonder what's under all of this?" I ask. "Before the coral, before the palace. Before the gods."

"The Hollow," Tarek says, half-joking. "The Drains tell stories about tunnels beneath the capital, where the first merfolk hid from Navedia's storm."

I turn toward him. "You believe that?"

"I believe stories don't last unless they want to be remembered."

The way he says it makes me think of Damon. His warning lingers—*the sea has more than one will.* It's the kind of line that burrows into you, growing sharper the longer you hold it.

"Tarek," I say quietly, "what if the sea isn't angry with me? What if it's just... different?"

He tilts his head. "Different how?"

"I don't know. It feels like I'm made of something it doesn't understand."

He studies me for a long moment, his expression unreadable. "Maybe the sea doesn't have to understand you to need you."

A sudden rush of current sweeps through the overlook, tugging at our hair and sending loose shells spinning. I brace myself against the railing. The water turns colder—an unnatural chill that seeps into my bones.

Then, just as quickly, it's gone.

Tarek glances upward. "Storm Current," he says softly. "I thought that died out generations ago."

"Maybe it's just the weather changing."

"Maybe." But he doesn't sound convinced.

Far above, lightning flickers faintly through the Light Veil. A pulse of brightness, then darkness, then brightness again. The surface storms rarely reach this deep, but sometimes their energy seeps down in strange ways. The Flowed call it the sea remembering the sky.

I watch until the flashes fade, leaving trails of silver behind my eyelids. "When I was little," I tell him, "Mother said the ocean was alive, like a body. The tides were its breathing, the currents its heartbeat. But if that's true, what are we?"

"Cells," he says. "Tiny ones that think they matter."

"That's bleak."

"Accurate, though."

We both laugh, the sound small in the wide water.

Then a ripple moves through the coral below us—faint but visible. The branches bend slightly, light traveling along them in a line that disappears into the distance.

"The Flow network," Tarek says, watching the glow fade. "That's how the palace sends energy through the city. It runs beneath every district, connecting the guilds. My father helped carve part of it."

"The Pulse beneath the Pulse," I murmur.

He looks at me sideways. "What?"

"Nothing." I shake my head. "It just... felt like something was listening."

He laughs. "Paranoid much?"

"Probably."

But as he walks ahead, I linger one last moment at the railing. The coral below no longer glows, but the faint impression of its light stays in my vision. It looked like a pattern—spirals nested within spirals, branching like veins. The same shape as the royal crest.

The same shape that appeared in the sand the day I touched the coral ring and killed its light.

The thought unsettles me enough that I push away from the overlook and follow Tarek back toward the palace. The water grows warmer as we near the inner courtyards, scented with kelp blossoms and salt-fruit from the market gardens above.

At the gate, he pauses. "You should rest that shoulder."

"I will."

"Liar."

"Compulsive," I say, smiling despite myself.

He rolls his eyes and swims off toward the Forgeborn quarters, leaving a faint trail of golden shimmer in his wake.

When I reach the royal wing, the guards bow but don't meet my eyes. I can tell the story of the training accident has already spread. The way they look at me now—half pity, half superstition—confirms what the court will whisper by nightfall: the Stillborn Tide has struck again.

I pass through the atrium lined with glowing mosaics of the gods. Their faces are serene, their eyes made of pearl and lightstone. Navedia, the exiled one, is absent from the row, his alcove sealed by a slab of coral too thick to see through. I've always wondered what they covered up.

As I drift past, the water shifts again—subtle, like breath against the back of my neck. For a moment, the sealed coral slab glints faintly blue.

Then the light fades, and I'm alone with the stillness.

When I finally reach my room, I lie back against the kelpwoven couch and close my eyes. The ache in my shoulder returns, sharper now, but beneath it is something stranger—a flicker of warmth spreading outward, threading through my veins.

The sea beyond my window glows with quiet light. The city's currentways pulse far below, constant, unbroken. And somewhere deeper, beyond all that order and rhythm, something vast and electric stirs—almost like it's turning over in its sleep.

CHAPTER FOUR

The Drift

The first light of festival morning slides through my window in long ribbons of gold, striping the walls and settling across my skin. Even from here, I can hear the city awakening—currents quickening, shells ringing as market stalls open, the faint rise and fall of distant hymns drifting from the Tide temples.

The Festival of Drift.

Even the name sounds lighter than most days in Lurea. It's the one time of year when the guilds pause their rivalries, when the Depth Council pretends to love the monarchy again, when the sea itself feels less like a weight and more like a song.

I sit up slowly, hair floating around me like a dark cloud. My shoulder aches from yesterday's training, but I ignore it. The ache feels smaller today. Manageable.

Mother says the festival began as a promise—an ancient pact between the six divine currents and the first Sea King, meant to remind us that harmony keeps the sea alive. Each citizen releases an orb into the current at dusk, glowing with their guild's color. The orbs drift together, merging light with light, until they vanish into the deep.

It's meant to be beautiful. It's meant to remind us we're all one.

But I can't help thinking about the ones who aren't invited to drift—the Drains, whose color, blue, is banned from every festival lantern. Their orbs would never reach the capital. Their light was declared unnatural centuries ago.

I rise from bed and stretch until my joints pop softly. My reflection in the mirror-pool wavers. The bruise from Zeke's current is gone, leaving only a faint shimmer that catches the light like dust. I smooth my scales, pull on the ceremonial wrap hanging from the wall—a thin coral-pink fabric that floats around me in gentle waves. The palace has rules about appearances during festival season. Royalty must shine. Even if it's only for show.

When I emerge into the corridor, Saphra is already waiting, arms crossed, her hair tied with tiny glowing shells. "You're late," she says, grinning. "Mother's in the atrium. Father's in a mood."

"When isn't he?"

"True." She loops her arm through mine, pulling me along. "I told her I wanted to wear the Bloom colors again, but she said the Queen's children represent unity, not preference. I said that sounds like a very boring way to live."

I laugh under my breath. “And what did she say to that?”

“She said I sounded like you.”

“Poor her.”

Saphra snorts and squeezes my arm. “Maybe she likes us that way.”

We turn into the main hall, where coral lanterns line the walls, casting slow-moving patterns across the floor. Servants move gracefully through the water, carrying trays of blossoms and polished pearls, each meant for the day’s offerings. The scent of kelp wine and sea jasmine mingles with the tang of currentstone dust.

The palace always feels alive before a celebration—like it’s exhaling after holding too much inside.

Mother stands near the lower steps of the throne platform, her back to us. She’s dressed in pale silver, her coral lungs glowing faintly through the thin fabric. The light within her moves with her breathing, rhythmic and beautiful. She turns when she hears us approach.

“There you are,” she says, smiling softly. “Both of you. Perfect timing. Come—let me see.”

Saphra twirls in the water. “Do I look like a future Queen?”

Mother tilts her head. “You look like someone who has jellyfruit stains on her sleeves.”

Saphra gasps. “Traitor!”

“Go find your brother,” Mother says, laughing. “Tell him to stop hiding near the training decks and come presentable.”

Saphra zips away, her laughter echoing through the hall like bells.

Mother's smile fades as she turns to me. "You're pale," she says.

"I'm fine."

She studies me for a moment longer. "Your father asked that you stay close tonight. No wandering."

"I wasn't planning to."

"Good. The Council will be watching the family closely this year. There's unrest among the Flowed guilds. Too many whispers about the trenches and what lies there."

I hesitate. "About the Drains?"

"Among other things." She looks past me, her gaze distant. "The sea is changing. I can feel it. The Pulse runs strange lately—out of rhythm."

"You sound like Damon."

"That boy reads too much."

"He's right sometimes."

She gives me a sharp glance, half warning, half affection. "So are you." Then she softens. "Don't worry about politics today. The Festival belongs to the people. Let yourself enjoy it. Please."

I nod, though enjoyment feels like something I forgot how to do. Still, I want to try.

After Mother leaves, I stay in the hall longer than I should, letting the light from the coral lanterns wash over me until my reflection vanishes into it. Around me, the palace stirs with the quiet excitement that always comes before ceremony—the sound of scales brushing silk, the clink of pearl jewelry being fastened, attendants whispering rehearsed greetings to themselves.

Saphra darts through a side corridor, clutching a bundle of ribbons, her veil slipping crooked over one eye. "Don't tell Mother," she says breathlessly, "but I traded the bloom garland for tide crystals. They sparkle more."

"You're supposed to wear green."

"Green is for healers." She twirls once, the ribbons fanning out behind her like a spray of light. "Maybe the sea will change its mind if I ask nicely."

I smile in spite of myself. "That's not how the sea works."

"It is for me." She disappears around the corner before I can argue.

I move slower through the corridors, tracing my fingers along the engraved coral walls. Every inch of this place tells the story of someone else's glory—battles fought, alliances sealed, blessings given by gods who no longer answer. I wonder if the sea remembers all of it, or if it forgets like we do, letting each age sink under the next.

Servants cross in front of me carrying stacks of lanterns, their faces flushed from the heat of the current engines that power the palace lights. The smell of saltfruit and warm metal hangs thick in the water. Somewhere in the distance, a choir practices the Drift hymn, their voices weaving through the currents like strands of silk.

I pause at one of the balcony arches that overlook the city. Lurea is already glowing in preparation. Banners ripple between coral spires, every guild color represented—except blue. Always except blue. The memory of that absence catches in my throat.

Behind me, Zeke's voice breaks the silence. "You're supposed to be dressing."

I turn. He's already in his ceremonial armor, plates of polished pearl bound with tideglass, light moving through it in waves. He looks older like this, every inch the future King they want him to be.

"You look ready," I say.

"Mother made sure of it." He studies me, expression softening. "You seem... better today."

"Define better."

"Not planning to run."

"I thought about it," I admit. "But the palace guards might get suspicious if I swim toward the Trench in festival silk."

He almost smiles. "Don't joke about that down here."

"I'm not joking."

We fall into silence, watching the city pulse below. He sighs. "Just stay close tonight. Please. Father's nerves are already stretched thin."

"As if I could do anything right enough to ease them."

Zeke looks at me then, really looks, and there's something in his eyes—regret, maybe. "It's not about right. It's about peace. He just wants to get through one celebration without scandal."

"Then he should've thought twice before marrying a human," I say, but softly, not cruelly.

He winces, and for a moment I regret it. "You sound like the Council."

"I sound like someone who knows what everyone else whispers when they think I can't hear."

"Maren—"

"It's fine," I say, cutting him off. "Let's just get through the night."

He nods once and leaves me at the balcony. I watch his light fade down the hall until I'm alone again.

The choir's song drifts nearer now, clear and slow. *Let the sea carry us / let the tide renew us / let all currents flow as one*. The words are old—older than the palace, older than the kingdom itself. They were written when the ocean still believed harmony could last forever.

I press a hand to my chest and feel my heartbeat answer, steady, defiant. The ache in my shoulder has faded, but in its place lingers something else: a tingling warmth that won't disappear. I breathe through it until the feeling dulls.

In the great hall below, servants hang the final lanterns, each one shaped like a pearl bloom and lit from within by the guilds' collective currents. The ceiling glows brighter with every light added, until the palace looks like the inside of a living reef. I catch a glimpse of Father at the far end, conferring with the Depth Council representatives. Their gestures are clipped, their smiles strained. Even now, politics finds its way into celebration.

I turn away, my stomach twisting.

Somewhere nearby, someone laughs—clear, high, unguarded. It's the kind of sound I used to make before

I learned how much could be taken from a single mistake.

I try to hold onto it, to remember how it felt to move without apology.

The hours drift like slow tides. The palace fills with guests—nobles in bright scales, guild leaders in their ceremonial armor, attendants weaving through the currents with trays of golden drink. I stand near the outer balcony, where the Light Veil glows faintly above, visible even from this depth. It looks like the surface is breathing.

Below, the city swells with movement. Processions wind through the streets, children carrying lanterns shaped like shells and coral blooms. Every building is draped in kelp banners, shimmering with guild symbols. Lurea looks alive in a way it rarely does—a symphony of color and motion.

"Do you think it's true?" a voice says behind me.

I turn. Neris floats at the edge of the balcony, her veil of white fabric trailing behind her. Her guild mark—the light sigil of the Lumehands—glows faintly on her wrist.

"Do I think what's true?" I ask.

"That the orbs carry pieces of us. That when they merge, the sea remembers us as one."

"I don't know."

"You should," she says, smiling faintly. "The royal line is supposed to keep faith alive."

"I think faith is louder when it's quiet," I answer.

Her smile falters. "That's a very dangerous thing to say."

"So I've been told."

She studies me for a moment, her expression unreadable. "You're different lately," she says finally. "There's something in your eyes. Like you're listening to a song no one else can hear."

Before I can respond, Father's voice echoes through the grand hall. "It's time."

The crowd stills. Even the water seems to settle, expectant.

Mother takes her place beside him, regal as a statue carved from light. Zeke and Saphra stand just behind, perfect portraits of royal grace. I move to join them, adjusting the coral wrap around my shoulders.

Father's gaze sweeps the assembly. "For generations, the Festival of Drift has reminded us of unity," he says, voice carrying through the water like a steady current. "Each orb we release honors the harmony between guild and crown, between tide and trench. Tonight, as our ancestors did, we offer our light to the sea."

Applause ripples through the hall. Servants bring forth the ceremonial orbs—smooth spheres of crystal, faintly luminous. Each one is filled with a thread of energy drawn from its bearer's current. Mine, as always, is faint.

Mother presses her hand over mine as I take it. "The sea sees the heart, not the strength," she whispers.

I nod, though my stomach twists.

We follow the procession out of the palace and into the open expanse above the city. Thousands of merfolk have gathered, their lights glowing in concentric circles that spiral outward into the dark. It's breathtaking—

the ocean alive with radiance, every color shimmering in motion.

A priest signals the beginning of the release. One by one, orbs drift upward, carried by the currents. Golds of Pressure, greens of Bloom, silvers of Tide, violets of Light. They swirl together, spinning slowly toward the horizon like stars reborn.

I hold mine longer than I should. The surface of the orb feels warm, almost pulsing. I whisper the old prayer under my breath, words taught to every child: *May my light find the flow. May it drift toward harmony.*

Then I let go.

The orb floats from my hands, rising with the others. For a moment, I feel lighter—like maybe the sea forgives.

But then mine veers.

It drifts sideways, away from the royal ring, away from the current entirely. I blink, confused, watching it tumble lower, slower, until it collides with another orb—one glowing blue.

The color shouldn't exist. It hasn't for centuries. Blue means exile. Blue means Drain.

The two orbs touch, and the world pauses.

A flash of light bursts outward—white, electric, searing through the water. My chest seizes. The glow races up my arms, scattering through my wrap, through the currents themselves. For a heartbeat, everything in Lurea blazes.

Then darkness.

The coral towers dim. The current highways flicker out. The sea itself seems to inhale.

Gasps ripple through the crowd. Someone screams. I hear Saphra cry my name.

The blue light fades, leaving nothing behind but two shards of glass tumbling toward the seafloor.

“Get her inside!” Father’s voice cuts through the panic. Guards rush forward, surrounding me, their armor gleaming faintly in the residual glow. The air feels charged, every breath sharp, metallic.

Mother pushes through them, grabbing my arm. Her fingers are cool, trembling. “Come,” she says. “Now.”

I can’t move at first. My body feels weightless, detached. “I didn’t—”

“Don’t speak.”

She pulls me through the chaos, her coral lungs flaring bright under her skin as if reacting to the same energy that just tore through me. The streets below are alive with confusion—merfolk darting in every direction, lights sputtering, the Flow pathways glitching with bursts of static.

We reach the palace gates. The guards close them behind us with heavy groans of coral and metal. Inside, the corridors glow weakly, the currentstones flickering. The whole kingdom feels like it’s holding its breath.

Mother doesn’t stop until we reach her private chambers. She seals the door and turns to me, eyes wild. “Did you touch it? The blue orb?”

“It touched mine.”

She closes her eyes. “That’s not possible.”

“It happened.”

Her hand trembles as she reaches toward me, pressing her palm flat to my chest. The moment she does, a spark jumps between us—small, but real. She pulls back sharply.

Her expression changes.

“Heartwake energy,” she whispers. “It’s in you.”

“I didn’t mean—”

“This isn’t your fault.” Her voice softens, but her eyes dart toward the door. “They’ll come soon. The Council will call it an omen. They’ll say the prophecy—”

She stops herself.

“What prophecy?” I ask.

Her mouth opens, then closes. “Not now. It’s only a story. Old superstition.”

“Mother.”

She grabs my shoulders. “Listen to me. Until I say otherwise, you don’t leave this room. You don’t speak to anyone about what happened. Not your father, not Zeke, no one.”

“What’s happening to me?”

She looks at me for a long time, her expression caught between awe and fear. “I don’t know,” she admits. “But the sea has chosen to wake something—and it used you to do it.”

Her words settle into me like a weight I can’t lift.

Outside, the city’s lights begin to flicker back to life, one by one. The Flow reactivates, threads of gold weaving once more through the coral streets. But the air feels different now—sharper, charged, alive in a way it wasn't before.

Mother presses her forehead against mine. "Whatever you are, Maren," she whispers, "don't let them name it before you do."

I nod, though my throat feels tight.

When she leaves, the room dims. I drift to the window and look out over Lurea. From here, the city glows unevenly, patches of darkness still lingering like bruises on its surface.

Somewhere far below, near the Trench, a faint blue shimmer answers back. It pulses once, twice, in perfect rhythm with my heartbeat.

CHAPTER FIVE

The Verdict

"...You would send your own blood into the dark!"

Mother's voice cuts through the chamber, sharp enough to slice the water. The coral walls shudder faintly under her words. The chamber's glow dims and brightens in uneven bursts, reacting to the rising tempers of those within.

The Depth Council is seated in a half-circle before the throne, seven elders cloaked in their guild colors. Pressure gold, Bloom green, Tide silver, Shadow gray, Light violet, Flux blue-green, and at the center—the empty chair of the Drains, unclaimed for centuries.

I stand near the rear, where shadows from the coral pillars stripe across my skin. The air feels too thin here, too shallow for breathing. They've been arguing for what feels like hours, but I stopped hearing words long ago. What remains is tone: accusation, fear, disgust.

"You saw what happened at the festival," says Councilor Varyn of the Tide Guild. His voice is slow and deep, like moving stone. "The current dimmed for the first time in living memory. The sea itself recoiled. That girl's presence—"

"My daughter's presence," Mother snaps.

"—is an omen," he finishes, undeterred. "The old prophecies speak clearly of a Sparkblood. The sea will not hold her peaceably."

"Prophecies," she repeats, spitting the word. "Stories told by fearful men who mistake evolution for blasphemy."

Across from him, the Bloom Guild's representative—a thin woman with coral branches threaded through her hair—raises her hand. "We're not here to debate myth. We're here to address the fact that the royal heir nearly collapsed the Pulse network last night. Half the city went dark. Coral crops in the lower district have wilted. My guild's healers are overrun."

My stomach knots. I glance down at my hands. They're steady now, but I can still feel the faint crackle beneath my skin. It's like a reminder of what I am—something volatile, barely contained.

"She didn't collapse the network," Mother says, her tone trembling at the edges. "It was a surge. The Flow corrected itself."

"After three hours," another councilor mutters.

Father's voice rises then, weary but commanding. "Enough."

The chamber stills. Even the water quiets, thick with the echo of authority.

He stands beside the throne, every inch the King of Tides—back straight, crown glinting like a captured wave. But I know that stance. It's not strength. It's endurance.

"She is neither cursed nor blessed," he says. "She is my daughter. And she will not be treated as an enemy of the sea."

"Your Majesty," Varyn says carefully, "your compassion does you credit, but compassion cannot anchor the tides. The people have seen what happened. The Council must act before faith erodes entirely."

"And what would you suggest?" Father asks. "Banishment? A royal execution? We are not savages."

"We propose exile," says the Bloom Guild leader. "To the Drains' territory. There, her... current cannot disrupt the Flow."

The words hit me harder than I expect. Exile. To the Trench. Among the outcasts who can barely breathe in the capital's light. My pulse stutters.

Mother's expression sharpens into fury. "You would cast her out like waste? You forget who built this kingdom—whose blood bought its peace. The first Sea King promised unity, and yet here you are, begging for segregation dressed as salvation."

A murmur ripples through the council seats.

Another elder leans forward, his skin pale with age, eyes bright as cut glass. "Unity has always required balance, Your Majesty. And balance sometimes demands sacrifice."

Father's jaw tightens. "You speak as though you understand sacrifice."

The silence that follows is deep enough to feel.

When he speaks again, his voice is quieter. "I will not exile her. And I will not confine her to the Vault."

"You cannot protect her from what she is," one councilor says.

"I can protect her from you."

Mother's hand touches his arm, but it's not comfort—it's a warning. "Thalen, be careful. They smell blood in the water."

His voice hardens. "My decision stands."

The council erupts in argument, their colors bleeding together into a chaotic swirl. The coral light dims again, flickering under the pressure of their raised voices.

I try to step back, but my shoulder brushes one of the pillars. A crackle runs through the stone, faint but visible. The nearest councilor notices. His eyes widen. "Did you see that?"

Mother moves fast. "It's the chamber's charge. The energy conduits are unstable."

But I see the truth in Father's eyes: he saw it too. The current that slipped from me. The surge.

"Enough for today," he declares, voice sharp. "This meeting is adjourned. The Council will reconvene after I've consulted with the Guildmasters privately."

The elders rise, each offering stiff bows that feel more like insults. As they drift toward the exit, their murmurs trail behind them like oil.

The prophecy.

The Sparkblood.

She'll undo us all.

Navedia's heir.

When the last of them leaves, the chamber feels cavernous. Only family remains.

Mother turns to Father. "You promised to protect her."

"And I am," he says.

"By letting them dissect her like a specimen? 'Further testing,' Thalen? That's what they'll call it. That's what you just agreed to."

"I agreed to buy her time."

Her eyes flash. "You're buying loyalty, not safety. You're always trying to appease the sea, as if faith can hold back fear."

He exhales, shoulders sinking. "You think I wanted this? You think I wanted my daughter to be born under still water, her first breath a warning?"

I flinch. The words slip from him before he can stop them. His regret shows in the slow closing of his eyes.

"Thalen," Mother whispers, broken.

"No," I say quietly. "Let him finish."

They both turn to me. My voice surprises even myself—steady, sharp. "You're all so busy deciding what I mean to the sea that you've forgotten to ask what the sea means to me."

"Maren—"

"I never asked for this," I continue. "I never asked to be born in a kingdom that thinks I'm a mistake. If the sea really wanted perfection, maybe it shouldn't have chosen a human for its queen."

Mother's breath catches, but it's Father who looks gutted. "Watch your tone."

"Why? You made this, didn't you? All of it. You and your holy marriage, your divine experiments. You fell in love with a human, Father. You broke your own laws. And I'm the one who has to pay for it."

He opens his mouth, but no sound comes out. The Crown Wave behind him—an arc of suspended water that mirrors his emotional control—shivers. Droplets fall from its edge, scattering like glass.

"Enough," he says finally. But it's not a command. It's a plea.

Mother's eyes glisten. She takes a step toward me, but I pull away. "Don't," I say. "I know you think this is about saving me, but it isn't. It's about proving you were right."

She looks as if I struck her. "Maren..."

Zeke speaks, his voice low. "She's not wrong."

Father turns sharply. "What did you say?"

Zeke's expression is unreadable. "You told me faith anchors us, but I think you're the one drowning in it. The Council isn't loyal to the sea—they're afraid of it. And maybe you are too."

"Careful, son."

"No," Zeke says. "I've been careful my whole life." He glances at me, and something passes between us—an understanding, fragile but real. "You taught us that the sea's will is absolute. But what if the sea's will is changing?"

Father's gaze hardens, but the Crown Wave flickers again, weaker this time. His faith, the one thing I thought unbreakable, is cracking.

Mother steps forward, her voice soft but firm. "The world is not ending, Thalen. It's evolving. The Pulse is shifting because it must. The ocean breathes, and right now, it's taking a new kind of breath."

He looks away. "You speak like the Drains."

"Maybe they're the only ones still listening."

Silence. Then, quietly, "This discussion is over."

He turns and leaves, the wave behind him settling into dull stillness.

For a long time, no one moves.

When he's gone, Mother releases a breath she'd been holding. "He'll come around," she says, though her tone wavers. "He has to."

Zeke shakes his head. "He's not hearing you anymore. He's hearing the priests. The Council."

"He's hearing fear," I say. My throat feels tight, like something alive is pressing against it. "And fear always wins here."

Mother looks at me, eyes wet. "Then we have to make something louder than fear."

I want to believe her. I want to believe the sea could forgive what it's never understood.

But as I leave the chamber, the faint crackle in my chest returns, small and steady, like a warning.

Outside the council chamber, the water feels thick and heavy, each movement dragging through it like swimming through thought. I don't look back. The echo of their voices still clings to the coral behind me—*exile, confinement, prophecy*—all of it circling like a storm I can't outswim. My hands ache from keeping them still.

I push through the corridor until the light shifts from the pale green of the council hall to the warmer golds of the main passage. I don't realize how fast I'm moving until I brush a current too sharply and a trail of disturbed bubbles follows behind me like a comet's tail. My chest tightens, a pulse thrumming unevenly under my skin.

"Running from ghosts or guilt?"

The voice drifts from a nearby archway, casual, amused.

Tarek lounges against a coral column, his copper-and-slate tail flicking lazily through the water. He's all confidence and ease—muscle and mischief wrapped in guild armor polished just enough to irritate his superiors.

"Neither," I say, slowing a little. "Just swimming."

"Fast enough to make the kelp bend backward," he says, grinning. "Let me guess. Council meeting went about as well as expected?"

"Worse."

"Ah." He pushes off the column with a flick of his fin, gliding beside me. "So, total disaster, then."

"Something like that."

We drift through the passage together, weaving around lantern pillars and the open lattice windows where light filters through the sea in wavering stripes. The palace gardens bloom faintly below, their coral spires stretching upward like fingers chasing the glow.

“Your father looked like he was ready to crush a pearl in his fist,” Tarek says. “And your mother—well, if looks could turn coral to ash...”

I sigh. “They’re still fighting about what to do with me. The Council thinks I’m an omen.”

“I think they’re idiots.”

“That’s comforting.”

“It’s true. You could make the sea boil and they’d still find a way to turn it into a sermon.”

A smile tugs at my mouth before I can stop it. “Careful. That’s borderline heresy.”

“Then I’ll drown happy.”

We pass through a tunnel of living coral, its edges lined with translucent sea fans that flutter in the current. The water here tastes faintly of saltfruit and oil from the lantern pods—clean, alive.

“You should’ve seen their faces,” I say. “Half of them wanted to exile me to the Trench. The other half wanted to lock me beneath the palace.”

“And your father?”

“Promised more testing.” I let out a brittle laugh. “Apparently, that’s love now.”

Tarek’s fin flicks in irritation, stirring up a small cloud of glittering silt. “You’re not an experiment, Maren.”

“Tell that to them.”

He glances over, studying my expression. “I’d rather tell it to you.”

We float in silence for a moment. Outside the windows, schools of lanternfish thread between coral towers, their bodies flashing in synchronized light. The city hums below us—alive, ordinary, oblivious to the storm in the palace.

Tarek leans back, crossing his arms behind his head. "You know what I'd do if they exiled me?"

"Run?"

He grins. "Run fast enough they'd have to rewrite the laws to catch me."

I snort. "You'd make a terrible fugitive. You'd stop for snacks halfway to the Trench."

"Only if the snacks were good."

The small laugh that slips out of me is the first real one I've managed all day. It feels strange in my throat, fragile, like it might break if I hold it too long.

"Better," he says quietly. "You needed that."

I shake my head, tail sweeping lazily through the water. "You always do that."

"Charm you?"

"Distract me."

"Same thing."

The warmth of the moment softens something in me, loosening the knot of anger that's been sitting under my ribs since the Council's vote. "They talk about balance and harmony like it's something fragile," I say. "But it isn't. The sea doesn't care who loves who. It doesn't care what blood flows in its depths."

"Then maybe the problem isn't the sea," Tarek says.

I look at him, meeting his gaze. "Then what is?"

He hesitates, the joke gone from his tone. "The people who pretend to speak for it."

The current drifts between us, slow and sure. I stare out over the city again—the coral domes glowing, the distant glimmer of the Light Veil high above. Everything looks perfect, untouched. It's the kind of beauty that hides rot underneath.

"I never asked for this," I say finally. "Not the bloodline, not the prophecy, not any of it. If anyone's to blame, it's my father for falling in love with someone who didn't belong here."

Tarek's tail stills, his expression softening. "That's not on you."

"It feels like it is."

He shakes his head, drifting closer. "You're not a mistake, Maren. You're proof that the sea can change. And change is messy. The old ones just can't stand getting their fins ruffled."

A short silence stretches between us before he adds, almost shyly, "Besides, if they do send you to the Trench, I'll come visit. Someone's got to make sure you don't start a rebellion without me."

I smile, faint but real. "You'd hate it down there. No decent wine, no patience for sarcasm."

"I'd adapt."

"You?"

He grins. "You'd be surprised how well I look in outlaw lighting."

That earns another laugh—louder this time, startled and warm. It bursts free, scattering a small ring of bubbles around us. The tension in my chest eases just a little more.

When I finally calm, Tarek is watching me with that lopsided smile again, one fin flicking lazily to keep him balanced. "There," he says. "Proof you're still capable of joy. Don't let them take that too."

For a moment, I just float there, caught between exhaustion and gratitude. The world feels almost kind again.

Then the water shifts, carrying the distant toll of the palace bells—three low notes that ripple through the current. Evening call.

Tarek sighs. "Guess that's my cue. Try not to overthrow the monarchy before breakfast."

"I'll do my best."

He salutes, a lazy wave of his tail sending him gliding away down the corridor, leaving a spiral of stirred sand in his wake.

I watch until he disappears around the bend. The silence that follows isn't lonely this time—it's steady. Balanced.

I turn back toward the glass, my reflection caught between the light of the city and the darkness of the deep.

CHAPTER SIX

The Experiment

The lesson is supposed to be about composure.

"Royalty is stillness," the tutor drones, a patient eel of a woman whose silver scales flash when she disapproves. "We are the calm between storms. A ruler's heart must never quicken before her people's."

I sit in the council chamber, spine straight, palms resting politely on my knees, pretending to listen. Every syllable floats past me like sand stirred by a current. The water feels too still in here—too measured, too neat. My pulse, on the other hand, has never learned obedience.

She's explaining the etiquette of diplomatic greetings now, her voice the steady trickle of a stream I'd like to dam. I glance toward the window slit where the outer currents shimmer faintly with light. The city is waking up again after the blackout, the Pulse lines along the coral streets blinking back into rhythm one by one.

It should comfort me. It doesn't.

Zeke sits a few paces away, feigning interest far better than I ever could. His tail flicks once, controlled. He's always been able to perform serenity. I was born too loud for that.

When the tutor calls my name for the next demonstration, the chamber door opens. A servant drifts in, eyes wide, voice low. "Her Majesty requests the Princess's presence in the lower wing. Immediately."

The tutor frowns. "We're in session."

"She said *now*."

Zeke's gaze flicks to mine. There's something sharp there—concern, maybe—but I ignore it. I'm already rising. The servant doesn't wait for permission; he gestures for me to follow and vanishes down the corridor.

The halls grow darker the deeper we swim, the walls sweating faint light through the coral seams. I know this route. I shouldn't. The laboratory lies beneath the palace heart, near the old tidal pumps that regulate the Pulse flow. Only the Queen and her most trusted aides are allowed here.

The servant stops at a sealed door carved with old sigils that hum faintly when approached. He presses his palm to a glyph, murmuring a phrase I can't catch. The coral splits like lips parting for breath.

Inside, the light changes.

Mother stands at the center of the chamber, surrounded by a storm of glass vials and coral tubes.

The water hums faintly with vibration, faint trails of Heartwake energy running through the cracks in the floor. It looks less like a lab and more like a creature's heart, throbbing and alive.

She doesn't look up when I enter. "Close the door."

"Mother—"

"Now."

The coral seals behind me with a sigh. I can feel the weight of it pressing on my spine.

She finally looks at me then, eyes bright, almost feverish. "How do you feel?"

"Like I just left a very long lesson on pretending."

"Not your mood. Your body."

"Fine. Tired." I hesitate. "The lights have been flickering all morning."

Her lips press together. "Yes. The Pulse is unstable. The Council blames the Heartwake surge from the festival."

"Wasn't it?"

"No." Her voice sharpens. "That was you. It responded to *you*."

I take a slow breath. "So you called me here to lecture me too?"

She drifts closer, and I realize she's shaking. "I called you here because I found something. Proof that your current exists—it's simply... buried. Trapped under interference. The sea won't yield to it, but maybe the Heartwake will."

The words hit like a current against my ribs. "You're still experimenting?"

She moves toward the central table where a new apparatus waits—a delicate contraption of coral filaments and glass veins filled with luminous blue fluid. "This isn't another test," she says. "It's the one that matters."

"Mother, the Council already—"

"I don't care what they ordered." Her voice breaks. "I won't let them take you. If I can stabilize your current, they'll have no reason to exile you. They'll have to see what you are."

"What am I?" I ask quietly.

Her gaze softens, almost sorrowful. "A bridge. Between what the sea was and what it's becoming."

I want to believe her. I want to believe in anything. But the pulse in my chest is quickening, and the chamber smells faintly of metal and ozone.

She takes my hand, her fingers trembling. "Just a trace," she says. "Less than a drop. The Heartwake essence is pure now—distilled from the crystal veins below the Trench. It will harmonize with what's inside you."

"And if it doesn't?"

She hesitates, then smiles—a fragile, desperate thing. "It will."

The air between us thickens. My tail sways involuntarily, stirring small whorls in the water. The currents around the table respond, shifting like they're holding their breath.

Mother prepares the injector—slender glass tipped with coral. The liquid inside gleams brighter than any current I've ever seen, a living blue so vivid it makes the rest of the world dull around it.

She steadies my arm. "You're not afraid?"

"I'm tired of being afraid."

The needle pierces skin.

For a moment, nothing. Just a spreading warmth beneath the surface, a shimmer crawling up my wrist like frost. Then—

The warmth turns sharp.

It's as if lightning has found its way into my veins. My spine arches. The room bends. The coral floor beneath my tail fractures in a perfect circle of light.

"Mother!"

She's shouting something, her face a blur of motion through the strobing light, but I can't hear her. Sound vanishes. Only pressure remains—pressure and brilliance.

The glow explodes outward, jagged threads of blue fire snapping through the water. Glass vials shatter. Streams of Heartwake essence ignite, arcing between metal and coral. I can feel it moving through me, not like water but like breath—alive, erratic, wild.

Somewhere behind the chaos, Mother is trying to reach me. The air crackles, the seals along the lab's edges burst one by one. The water itself vibrates, alive with static.

"Let it go!" she cries, voice faint through the storm. "Breathe with it—don't fight!"

I can't tell if I'm breathing at all. My body is too bright to feel. Every nerve burns, every thought dissolves into light. I see flashes of the city above, towers flickering as their power lines falter. The Pulse corridors waver. The entire ocean seems to pause, like it's watching me.

Then, just as suddenly as it began, it stops.

The light collapses inward, sinking back into my skin. The water stills. My vision narrows to a single point—the faint glow of Mother's coral lungs, flickering in and out like a dying lantern.

When I look down, my own hands are glowing. Not gold, not white—blue.

The same forbidden color.

I try to speak, but the sound that comes out isn't a word—it's a ripple that moves through the water, lighting the edges of the broken coral.

Mother catches me before I fall. Her face swims above mine, eyes wide with both awe and terror.

"Maren... you're alive."

I blink, my skin still pulsing faintly with light. "It feels—different."

"It worked." Her voice cracks. "It *worked*."

The word feels wrong. Around us, the lab is wreckage—glass shards floating like dead jellyfish, coral conduits sparking faintly with leftover current. The palace trembles as the main power lines strain to reconnect. Somewhere above, I hear the dull groan of a gate shutting and a distant chorus of voices shouting in alarm.

The sea outside the windows is dark. Every lantern in Lurea has gone out.

Mother clutches my face, her breath coming in ragged pulls. "Stay still. The current needs to stabilize. If the Council senses the Pulse deviation—"

Her words dissolve into static. My body feels weightless, my heartbeat a distant echo.

Through the cracked glass above, the first rays of the Light Veil spill downward, pale and uncertain. The sea's glow feels fragile—like a heartbeat waiting for permission to start again.

And somewhere in that silence, I realize I can hear it. Not the sea. Not the Pulse. Something deeper.

Something calling my name.

When the palace lights finally flicker back to life hours later, the ocean's Pulse does not resume right away. The currents hesitate, as though the sea itself is deciding whether to continue.

And on the floor of the ruined laboratory, I open my eyes to find thin veins of blue lightning still dancing faintly beneath my skin.

At first, there's only the ache.

It radiates from my center outward—sharp at the start, then rolling, dissolving into heat that spreads beneath my skin. It's not like fire; it's colder, alive, a river of light threading through every part of me. I can feel it racing through the veins along my arms, curling through my spine, dancing across the edges of my tail.

I try to move, but the water around me resists. It feels denser now, thick with the taste of metal and something sweeter—ozone and salt and memory. My body thrums with it, too full to contain itself.

"Mother?" My voice comes out low and distorted, almost harmonic. I see the ripples it makes shimmer through the water, vibrating the broken shards of glass around me.

She's near, eyes wide, lips parted as if caught between prayer and disbelief. The coral embedded beneath her skin glows faintly in response to me, like her body is mirroring mine. "Don't move," she breathes. "It's— it's syncing."

I can't stop shaking. The current in me surges, then steadies, finding rhythm. My pulse no longer beats alone; it feels doubled, accompanied by something greater, something ancient. Every inch of me hums—not just with power but with awareness.

For the first time in my life, the water bends *for me.*

I raise my hand slowly. The currents answer, rippling outward from my fingertips in silver-blue arcs. The floating debris responds, orbiting me like small moons. My chest tightens, not in pain this time but awe.

"Is this—" My throat catches. "Is this what having a current feels like?"

Mother presses her palm to her mouth, tears clouding her eyes. "Yes," she whispers. "Yes, Maren. You found it."

But it doesn't feel found. It feels *unleashed.*

The ache turns to thrill, the cold into heat, the pressure into weightless euphoria. I feel everything at once—the subtle tremors of the sea, the soft creaks of the coral walls, the faint magnetic pull of the Pulse lines far above. They're alive. I can sense them stretching through the kingdom like veins.

The ocean isn't quiet anymore. It's *singing.*

My heartbeat matches it, steady at first, then quickening until I can't tell where I end and it begins.

The glow under my skin brightens until it hurts to look at.

"Breathe," Mother says. "You have to control it. Draw it inward, not out."

I try. I do. But the energy is restless. It surges through me with no regard for boundaries, swelling against the edges of my ribs, my throat, my fingertips.

The pain returns—only this time, it's not sharp. It's everywhere, a pressure that fills every hollow space inside me. My vision flickers with white, then blue. The water grows warmer.

"Mother," I gasp. "It's too much."

"Focus on me," she says, swimming closer. "Anchor to me, Maren. Listen to my voice."

I reach for her hand. Electricity leaps before I make contact, sparking between our palms. The force throws her back, her body tumbling into the coral wall.

"Mother!"

The power surges. It doesn't care about my fear—it *feeds* on it. Every emotion becomes fuel. The walls glow with veins of light, spreading outward from where I float. The water churns, pressure shifting wildly, compressing until the coral starts to crack.

I clutch my head. "Stop, stop—please—"

But the current is past stopping. It's as if the sea itself is trying to pour through me. My body arches, light spilling from my fingertips in jagged bolts that carve across the room. Instruments disintegrate in bursts of shards. The table splits clean down the middle.

Mother shields her face as the surge hits the ceiling. The current seals rupture one by one, releasing the compressed flow from the palace pumps. The sound is deafening—a deep, thrumming roar that shakes the entire chamber.

I scream, but the sound turns into another pulse of light. It bursts from my chest, tearing upward, striking the coral lattice above us. The walls explode in streams of glowing dust.

The water floods with shards of light and swirling darkness. My tail thrashes instinctively, the edges of my fins glowing with white-hot arcs. For one perfect, terrifying second, I can see *everything*.

The sea beyond the palace.

The Pulse veins connecting Lurea to the deep.

The trench below, flickering faintly with blue fire.

Something vast stirs there—something that *feels* me.

And then, like a breath held too long, the energy collapses inward.

My body goes rigid. The world folds in on itself—light imploding, pressure dropping so fast my ears pop. When it's over, silence rushes in, sudden and brutal. The only sound left is the slow crackle of residual sparks fading into the dark.

I drift weightless amid the ruin. The air smells scorched. My body feels both heavy and not mine. The pain is gone, replaced by a strange, electric numbness. I can still feel the current pulsing under my skin, quiet now, coiled, waiting.

"Mother?" My voice is hoarse, the word rippling weakly through the silence.

She's slumped near the far wall, breathing hard, her coral lungs flickering erratically. When she looks up, her expression is half awe, half horror.

"The Heartwake—" she whispers. "It heard you."

My reflection wavers in a shard of broken glass beside me. My eyes glow faintly blue, their light dimming with each beat of my heart.

I should feel afraid. I should feel broken. But all I feel is *alive*.

The water around me trembles, responding to my breath. I reach out, fingers brushing the current. It follows. The sensation is intoxicating—a slow, humming thrum that feels like belonging.

I'm not empty.

Somewhere deep inside, beneath the rush and the ruin, something whispers my name again—clearer this time, almost fond.

I exhale, and the faintest spark drifts from my lips, dissolving into the water like a secret.

The palace above still flickers in and out of darkness. The Pulse hasn't recovered. But I have. I can't feel my pain anymore. Only the charge.

Only the quiet, consuming certainty that I was never meant to flow with the sea. I was meant to *ignite* it.

CHAPTER SEVEN

The Girl

When I wake, the sea is screaming.

Not with sound, but with motion—currents tearing through the city in wild spirals, pressure shifting like a living creature thrashing in its sleep. The water feels wrong, heavy and fast, dragging at everything it touches. I can taste iron and salt on my tongue.

From my chamber window, Lurea no longer glows with order. Coral towers pulse in uneven bursts of light, their rhythm broken. Market canopies whip in the erratic tides, and below, the current highways that once flowed like arteries now clash and cross, colliding with each other in violent surges. Schools of fish scatter in confusion. Floating gardens are torn from their moorings, drifting into the upper reefs.

The chaos ripples through every layer of the city. In the distance, I see a bridge of woven kelp snap, its arch collapsing into a whirl of debris. Lantern orbs that once floated gently through the market now careen like falling stars, their casings cracking and spilling light into the dark. Merchants struggle to anchor their stalls as waves of displaced current slam against them, overturning baskets of fruit and spilling coils of shimmering fabric that drift like ghosts through the chaos.

The coral dwellings along the lower ring groan under the strain. Cracks split open along their sides, releasing clouds of plankton and shimmering dust. A family clings to the edge of a balcony, their tails thrashing as they fight the drag of a rogue undertow. Soldiers in pressure armor push through the swells, trying to restore the flow conduits, their luminous staffs dimming with every pulse.

Even the sea creatures behave strangely. A pod of rays circles low to the ground, their lights flickering in sync with the collapsing currents, while a lone serpent eel coils itself around a coral column, biting at the surface as if the very water has turned against it.

The rhythm of the ocean—the constant pulse I've felt my whole life—fractures. The water vibrates with wild, unpredictable energy. The city's hum, that deep comfort that underlies every breath, falters and breaks apart into discordant silence.

Then the palace itself begins to convulse. Coral seams split with sharp cracks, releasing trails of bubbles that spiral upward like blood in clear water. The great chandelier of the Hall of Flow detaches from its anchor and drifts sideways, crashing into a row of statues that once depicted the first rulers.

The floor beneath me quivers, a deep, resonant tremor that moves through the palace bones. The water shudders so violently I have to grab the edge of the window to keep from being thrown backward. A low boom reverberates through the corridors, distant but immense—something giving way far below.

A wave of displaced current surges upward from the lower districts, rattling the glass dome above my head. A rain of crushed shell and pearl dust drifts down around me, glittering in the fractured light.

Then, through the din, a voice rises from the courtyard below—panicked, sharp. "Find the Princess!"

And another answers, closer, desperate.

"Pulsebreak!"

I grab the edge of my bedpost to steady myself. The faint blue glow beneath my skin is dim now, but it flickers with every tremor, answering the chaos outside like an echo.

"Princess!" A guard bursts into the doorway, tail lashing wildly to stay balanced. "You need to stay in your chamber. The city is—"

"I can see it."

"His Majesty has ordered confinement in the upper wing. The Queen is... detained for questioning."

The words slam into me harder than the tremors. "Detained?"

He swallows. "The Council believes her experiments destabilized the Pulse. They're convening with the King now."

"Where?"

"Main audience hall, but—"

I'm already gone, gliding through the corridor before he can finish. The halls are chaos—servants clutching lanterns that flicker in and out, guards barking orders that vanish under the roar of shifting currents. A mural splits down the middle as a crack snakes through the coral wall. Water pressure hisses through it like a venting wound.

I pass a window slit and see the outer city tilting. Market domes are flooding as entire current channels reverse direction. Coral blooms along the lower streets glow too bright, feeding on the excess energy until their petals burst in clouds of glowing dust. It's beautiful and terrifying at once—the sea remaking itself without permission.

By the time I reach the audience hall, the King's voice rolls through the corridors like thunder. I pause at the threshold, hidden behind one of the carved pillars, my pulse stuttering in my throat.

"...this is her doing," he says, and even from here I can hear the tremor in his restraint. "Selara's interference with Heartwake essence was forbidden. You warned her, and still she defied you."

Mother's name cuts through me like a blade.

Councilor Varyn's reply comes, slow and sure. "Then the prophecy holds, Majesty. The Sparkblood has awakened, and the sea rejects her. We must seal her before the Pulse unravels entirely."

The silence that follows is heavy, suffocating.

Father speaks again, lower this time. "She is my daughter."

"Your daughter has fractured the ocean's flow," another voice insists—Bloom Guild, I think, sharp and brittle. "You heard the readings. The Pulse has hesitated. Whole sectors are dark. If we don't contain her power, the sea itself could still."

"She's not a weapon," Father says.

"Not yet," murmurs Varyn. "But she could become one."

The phrase sinks into me like weight.

"Then confine her," says another voice, one I don't recognize. "The Vault can contain divine energy. Seal her there until the currents restore balance."

"No," Father says, voice sharp again. "No daughter of mine will be caged like a criminal."

But the hesitation in his tone betrays him.

Varyn presses on. "Majesty, the Vault was built for this very purpose—for anomalies of divine resonance. We cannot risk the sea's collapse."

"Enough!" The word echoes through the chamber. The Crown Wave above the dais glows red, bleeding light across the room. "Do not speak of my child as if she were a disease!"

I close my eyes, gripping the pillar. The coral beneath my palm hums faintly. My heartbeat won't slow. I know this ending. They'll corner him until he yields, until they convince him I'm too dangerous to keep near the throne.

A hand catches my arm.

"Not the best time to eavesdrop," Tarek murmurs, appearing from the shadow of the corridor. His copper tail glints in the dim light, scales dulled by dust.

I start to speak, but he shakes his head. "I heard the same thing. They're going to seal you."

"My mother—"

"Already taken to the lower chambers." His voice is quiet, urgent. "They're calling it containment. The guards won't let you near her."

I try to move toward the doors anyway, but he blocks me with an arm. "Maren. Stop. You can't help her if you're locked in the Vault."

"Then what do you suggest?"

His eyes meet mine, steady and unflinching. "You disappear."

"I can't just—"

"You can." His grip tightens. "There's a maintenance tunnel below the east pumps. It leads out through the outer walls. The Council doesn't know it exists."

My tail flicks, stirring the dust in the water. "And after that?"

He shrugs, a ghost of a grin flickering across his face. "After that, we survive long enough to decide what comes next."

A deep vibration runs through the floor, shaking loose more shards of coral. The hall lights flare, then die entirely. For one breathless instant, Lurea is plunged into darkness.

Tarek's voice is a whisper near my ear. "That's our chance."

We move fast, cutting through the corridors like shadows. Without light, the palace feels alien—the architecture less divine, more skeletal. The silence is punctuated by the occasional groan of shifting stone, the distant thunder of broken currents colliding in the city below.

As we descend, the temperature drops. The air smells of old salt and iron. The pulse of the sea—usually constant—stutters like a dying heart.

We reach the tunnel hatch just as shouts echo down the hall behind us. Guards. The glow of their current seals flickers like firelight, growing closer.

Tarek curses under his breath, forcing the hatch open. “Go!”

I hesitate, glancing back once. Through the crack in the coral walls, I can see the faint blue shimmer still running beneath my skin. The same blue that ruined the festival, the same blue that brought the sea to its knees.

For a heartbeat, I wonder if the Council is right—if I am a danger, if the sea really does reject me. But then I remember my mother’s words: *Don’t let them name it before you do.*

I dive through the hatch.

Cold water floods my senses, thick and new. The tunnel slopes downward, carved from rough coral and metal veins that hum faintly beneath my fingertips. The current here is stronger, wild but alive. It carries me forward, away from the palace, away from the shouts fading behind us.

The deeper we go, the rougher the sea becomes. Stray currents clash in the narrow space, twisting our path into whirlpools that bite at our fins. The hum of the Heartwake energy pulses through the coral walls like a heartbeat out of rhythm—too fast, too erratic. My tail aches from the effort of steering through it. Tiny shards of stone drift in the water, glowing faintly with the residue of broken current seals.

Above us, the palace's silhouette fractures through the haze. Plumes of sand rise from the seabed as another shockwave passes through the foundation, bending metal and coral alike. I glance over my shoulder and see faint trails of light spiraling upward—the palace lights trying, and failing, to rekindle. For a heartbeat, the outline of the royal spire flashes brilliant gold before dimming again into darkness.

The tunnel walls groan, bending under the stress. Strips of coral peel away, revealing veins of molten blue current flickering beneath the surface. The air buzzes with static. I can *feel* it pressing against my skin, an invisible tide that wants to pull me backward, back to the source of the chaos I created.

Tarek reaches for my hand. His touch steadies me, grounding me as another tremor tears through the tunnel. Dust clouds rise from the ceiling, obscuring everything in a blur of gray and silver. Through the shifting water, I can hear the muffled sounds of the city still unraveling above—shouts, alarms, the hollow moan of collapsing structures.

"Keep close," he murmurs, voice low but clear. "The current's turning."

It is. The flow reverses suddenly, dragging us sideways into a spin. I press against the wall, my tail thrashing for balance, the coral rough beneath my palms. The tunnel feels alive, every inch of it trembling with the sea's distress. A faint whistle starts up—a high, keening sound that grows louder as we descend. The hum becomes vibration, then thunder, until it feels like the entire ocean is quaking around us.

A burst of light flashes behind us—white, then blue. The pressure slams into my back like a solid wave, throwing me forward. My shoulder scrapes the coral edge, but the water catches me before I collide with the wall. Tarek curses under his breath, the glow from his armor flickering.

“What was that?”

“The palace,” he says, breath unsteady. “Something just gave way.”

I twist around. Through a gap in the tunnel’s curve, I see it: a column of light erupting from the palace heart, spiraling upward through the sea like a pillar of fire. Even from here, I can feel its heat. The current bends around it, the water itself folding.

For a moment, all I can do is stare. That light—it feels like *mine.*

Tarek pulls at my wrist. “Don’t stop now.”

We push onward, the current surging faster, funnelling us through the last stretch of the tunnel. The walls smooth out, widening into a final corridor that feels almost ancient. The coral here glows faintly, etched with patterns that pulse as we pass, reacting to us. I recognize the symbols—older than the kingdom, relics of the first Pulse-builders.

The water shifts again, and the tunnel opens into a vast expanse beneath the city’s outer ridge. For a moment, the light blinds me.

When my eyes adjust, I gasp.

From here, Lurea stretches above us, silhouetted against the faint glow of the Heartwake deep below. The city looks fragile, suspended by light and faith. The once-stable currents twist around it in restless ribbons, brushing its edges like fingers testing glass for cracks. Whole sections of the lower ring are dark now, patches of the city swaying under the pull of the changing tides.

Even in ruin, it's breathtaking—like watching a god's creation coming undone.

He catches up beside me, breathing hard. "Still think you're cursed?"

I glance at the pale blue glow wrapping my hands like bracelets. "No," I say quietly. "I think I'm awake."

Behind us, the palace alarms ring through the water—long, low notes that tremble through the current like grief.

The ocean has lost its balance, and it's looking for someone to blame.

I flick my tail once and disappear into the dark.

CHAPTER EIGHT

The Edge

The water beyond the city feels heavier. Older.

It presses against me in a way the palace never did—cooler, ungoverned, wild. The current here doesn't hum in perfect rhythm or glide along clean-cut channels; it *breathes*. It surges and retreats, carrying silt and sand from places no one has mapped in centuries.

We've been traveling for what feels like hours, though time drifts strangely in the open sea. The last faint shimmer of Lurea has long since vanished behind a curtain of haze, its ordered glow swallowed by the expanse. All that remains is the faint shimmer of Tarek's lightstone tied to his belt and the pulsing trail of lantern kelp above us, like stars scattered across a night that never ends.

We hide among the caravan of nomadic traders—the Driftborn, they call themselves. A line of wide-shelled gliders pulls their floating wagons through the deep, coral lanterns hanging from long ropes. The air tastes different here, colder and sharper, rich with the metallic tang of minerals rising from the abyss below. The smell of smoked seaweed and fermented kelp fruit lingers around the caravan, mingling with the hum of conversation and the creak of rope against bone.

The Driftborn move like a single living thing, each trader's tail flicking in rhythm with the gliders' long, sweeping strokes. The sound of their movement is constant—a soft brushing, a rhythm of scales against current. The ropes that tether the wagons sway with the motion, creaking softly as if whispering to one another. Light spills from the lanterns, rippling across their faces in warm, honeyed waves. Everything about them feels rough and unpolished—free in a way the palace could never be.

I keep my head down, clutching the strap of a borrowed pack, the scent of salt and sun-bleached bone heavy in the fabric. The traders speak in dialects I barely understand—slurred, fluid versions of the language, shaped by deep-sea currents instead of royal halls. Their laughter carries in the water, bright and sharp, cutting through the lingering fear that still grips my chest.

I've never seen people move like this. They don't glide with the measured grace the palace tutors demand; they lunge and dart, shifting direction mid-sentence, chasing fish, sharing drink, fixing nets. Their bodies glitter faintly with bioluminescent paint—marks that identify their clans and trades. Some wear coral jewelry carved from the bones of long-dead leviathans. A few carry weapons fashioned from volcanic stone, humming with faint energy.

It feels like being inside a current—chaotic, beautiful, and untamed.

Tarek swims a little ahead, trading quiet nods with the caravan leader—a woman with scales black as volcanic glass and a scar that runs from her collarbone down the length of her tail. She glances at me once, her gaze sharp but not unkind.

For a moment, I wonder what she sees: a girl dressed in borrowed driftcloth, her movements too controlled, her eyes too polished by the palace. I'm trying not to look like what I am, but I can feel the difference—the stiffness of someone raised in still water.

Her eyes narrow slightly, as if reading my thoughts. "You're new to the deep," she says, her voice low and rough, carrying through the current like gravel dragged by tide.

"I've... never been this far out," I admit.

"Figures." She adjusts the rope in her hands, knotting it around a coral hook. "You move like someone expecting the water to ask permission first."

My face heats. "Does it show that much?"

She grins, revealing a row of sharp, polished teeth. "Only to those of us who've stopped asking."

Tarek hides a smile, flicking his tail toward me in quiet amusement. "Don't take it personally. The Driftborn test everyone they meet. It's how they measure truth."

"Truth?" I echo.

He nods. "They say the current always carries truth to the surface, no matter how deep you bury it."

The leader snorts. “That’s a poet’s way of saying we can smell liars.” She ties off the rope and drifts closer, circling me once. “You smell like kelp ink and fear. But also power. It’s an interesting mix.”

I flinch. “I didn’t mean to—”

“Relax, Sparkfish.” Her tone softens, though her eyes remain sharp. “I’m not judging. Just warning. The sea beyond this ridge doesn’t forgive easily. If you’re running from something, you’d better swim faster than its memory.”

I can’t meet her eyes. The glow beneath my skin has dimmed since we left Lurea, but I still feel it—quiet, restless, alive. Every time I breathe too deeply, it flares against my ribs, as though reminding me that I don’t belong here either.

The leader gestures toward the distant ridge, where faint lights flicker in the gloom. “We stop ahead to rest. Keep your heads down when we anchor. The Council has hunters near the northern current line. If they scent palace blood, we’re all in trouble.”

Tarek nods. “Understood.”

She tilts her head toward him, her scar catching the light. “And you—keep her steady. The sea eats the lost.”

Then she turns away, shouting orders to the other traders. Her voice rolls through the caravan like a pulse, and the group responds immediately, shifting formation.

I watch her go, my stomach tightening. *The sea eats the lost.*

The water around me doesn’t feel like a cradle. It feels like a living, breathing thing—and I’m not sure it wants me here.

Tarek glances back at me, his grin small but steady. "Don't let her scare you. The Driftborn exaggerate."

I manage a breath that's halfway to a laugh. "So we're not in danger?"

"Oh, we are," he says. "Just not from the sea."

His tone is light, but the glance he casts over his shoulder—to the horizon, where the faint shadow of Lurea still burns in the distance—tells me what he doesn't say. The real danger isn't the wild current or the deep. It's the world I left behind.

"Stay close to your shadow, palace girl," she says. "The open sea remembers faces it's not supposed to."

I pretend not to flinch at the word *palace.* It clings to me no matter how far I drift.

We stop near a ridge where the seabed dips into a vast canyon. The traders begin unpacking their wares—bundles of coral-thread fabric, jars of glowing plankton, relics scavenged from ruins swallowed by the tide. They anchor the caravan to a cluster of coral spires, each post pulsing faintly as the magnetic seals activate.

It's quieter here, though the water hums with movement. The ocean beyond the ridge looks endless, a dark expanse lit only by the occasional flare of bioluminescent creatures that glide through the deep.

I press a hand to my chest. The faint blue veins beneath my skin answer with a pulse—steady, almost calm. For now.

"First time outside the palace walls?" the merchant leader asks, floating beside me as she secures her pack.

I nod. "It's different."

"Different?" She smirks. "No. *Real.* The current here doesn't wait for orders. It eats them."

The words sink deep, settling somewhere between fear and wonder.

For as long as I can remember, the palace walls have muted the sea—every current regulated, every wave translated into gentle rhythm. This is nothing like that. Here, the water breathes hard. It growls. It feels *alive.*

A younger trader swims past, looping glowing wire around a broken anchor. He pauses when he sees me, eyes wide, lips parting as if he's about to speak. The scarred woman shoves him lightly. "Don't stare. She's not a ghost."

But the boy doesn't move. He whispers something under his breath—a word that makes the water around us still.

"*Sparkblood.*"

My stomach twists.

The woman's head snaps toward him. "Say that again, and I'll have you polishing eel teeth until next moon."

He bows quickly, retreating, but the damage is done. The word hangs between us, glowing faintly in the space it occupies.

She looks at me, unreadable. "You didn't hear that."

"I did."

"And you'd better forget it." She turns away, snapping a coil of rope between her hands. "Names like that don't float for free. They drown what carries them."

But the word follows me anyway, circling like a curious fish. *Sparkblood.* I can't tell if it feels like a warning or a prophecy.

Later, as the traders settle around their lanterns, I drift to the edge of the ridge. The seabed below stretches into darkness so deep it feels like it could swallow light itself. Somewhere far beneath, I glimpse faint blue fire flickering through the chasm—the Heartwake's glow, or maybe something older.

"The Drains live down there," Tarek says quietly, gliding beside me.

"You've seen them?"

"No one sees them. They stay in the Hollow, beneath the current lines. It's said the sea breathes differently there—too slow for the living, too fast for the dead."

"Sounds welcoming."

He gives me a crooked smile. "You'd fit right in."

I want to laugh, but the truth in his tone makes my chest ache.

The caravan begins to dim its lanterns, signaling rest. The glow fades until only the faint green shimmer of the ridge remains. I lean against a coral outcrop, letting the current wash over me. It's rougher here, unpredictable, laced with cold bursts that sting the skin. The water tastes raw, filled with minerals and life that hasn't been filtered by the city's machines.

And beneath it all, the Pulse stutters again.

At first, it's distant—like a faraway thunderstorm—but then it grows louder, closer. The water vibrates with it. The traders stiffen, murmuring quick prayers under their breath.

"Stormcurrent," one whispers.

Then the shadows move.

Shapes appear in the distance—sleek and armored, their armor flashing with the insignia of the Depth Council. The glow of their staffs cuts through the dark like knives.

Tarek grabs my wrist. "Guards."

"How did they—"

"Doesn't matter. Move."

The caravan erupts into motion. Traders scatter, cutting anchor lines and fleeing into the dark. The water fills with flurries of silt and broken light as the first shockwave hits, a surge of pressure that knocks me sideways. Coral cracks against my arm, leaving a trail of blood that swirls through the water like ink.

A voice rings through the current, distorted through an amplifier shell. "By order of the King and Council, surrender the exile known as Maren of Lurea."

I freeze. The name burns through me, raw and final.

Tarek positions himself between me and the approaching lights. "Keep your head down," he mutters.

The guards fan out, forming a crescent. Their weapons hum with contained current energy, the tips sparking white. The lead soldier raises a trident etched with Flow sigils. "Last warning."

The air tightens around me. The faint blue glow under my skin stirs, answering the threat before I can think. My pulse quickens—too fast, too loud. I can feel the electricity building, crawling up my arms like a living thing.

“Maren,” Tarek says, his voice sharp. “Don’t.”

“I can’t—”

The nearest guard lunges. Instinct overtakes fear. I throw out my hand.

The surge that leaves me is blinding. Blue light explodes through the water, cracking across the guards’ armor in jagged arcs. The shockwave ripples outward, bending the currents, snapping coral. Every lantern within reach bursts, showering the water with sparks.

The guards collapse in slow motion, their bodies convulsing as their lights flicker out.

The silence that follows is unbearable.

Tarek stares at me, wide-eyed, his tail barely moving. Around us, the water still shimmers with static, strands of energy drifting like smoke. My hands tremble, crackling faintly with leftover current.

The faint taste of metal coats my tongue.

“What did you do?” he whispers.

“I didn’t mean to.” My voice breaks. “I didn’t—”

But the words crumble. The truth sits heavy in my chest: for one small, terrifying moment, it felt good. It felt like control. Like belonging.

Now, it just feels like fear.

The guards float motionless, the last of their light fading into the dark.

Tarek grabs my wrist again, pulling me toward the canyon. “We have to move before they wake the current lines.”

I glance back once. The ridge glows faintly where the energy touched it, veins of blue crawling through the coral like wildfire. The water tastes different now—charged, restless.

Somewhere deep below, the Heartwake answers with a slow, pulsing flash.

The sea has felt me again.

CHAPTER NINE
The Darkness

The panic starts as a vibration—too deep to be heard, too heavy to ignore. It thrums through the water, shaking every bone in my body, until even the currents around us begin to tremble.

"Down!" Tarek shouts, his voice breaking through the chaos.

The world erupts.

A wall of pressure slams through the ridge, snapping coral spires like reeds. The Driftborn scatter, their gliders spinning out of formation as a roaring tide crashes from above. Light fractures into a thousand shards. The water turns to noise—rushing, breaking, swallowing everything.

Someone screams, a high sound swallowed by the deep. The ropes tethering the caravan whip loose. A lantern explodes in a burst of molten gold, sending molten light streaking across the sea. I feel it all at once: the sting of heat, the crush of current, the thundering beat of the sea gone wild.

Tarek's hand catches mine. "Hold—"

The surge hits again.

We're torn apart.

I'm thrown backward into darkness, spinning so fast I can't tell which way is up. The water burns my throat, my ears ring with pressure. The faint blue light under my skin flashes once, dim, then disappears.

Not now, I beg silently. *Please not now.*

I kick hard, but the current drags me down. The deeper I sink, the colder the water becomes—thin, metallic, full of ash. Shapes flicker in the dark: drifting wreckage, flashes of broken lanterns, silhouettes of bodies twisting in the current. My lungs ache, my tail is lead, and somewhere above me I think I hear Tarek calling my name, though it could just be the sea mocking me.

The pressure tightens around my chest. My vision flickers, edges darkening. I can't keep fighting the current. I can't keep—

Then, silence.

Not the calm kind—the heavy kind that follows collapse.

The water here is black, lit only by faint ribbons of molten light running through cracks in the seafloor. I drift, suspended between exhaustion and surrender. My heartbeat is a drum I can barely hear. For a moment, I let myself imagine the sea taking me back. Maybe this is what it wanted all along—to reclaim what shouldn't have existed.

Something moves in the dark.

I open my eyes just as the water around me shifts. Figures emerge from the black—shadows with glowing eyes, their tails long and scaled in patterns that catch faint blue light. They move silently, faster than I can react. Hands—cool, sure—grab my arms, my shoulders. I try to twist free, but I'm too weak to resist.

The last thing I see before the darkness folds over me again is the mark etched on their armor: a single, curling line of blue fire.

The symbol of the Drains.

The sight of it burned itself into my vision even as the darkness closed in—a single curling streak of blue fire, the same forbidden color that still throbbed beneath my skin. After that, everything dissolved. The world folded inward, water tightening like a fist. I remember hands—rough, scaled, sure—hauling me through the currents. I tried to speak, to ask who they were, where they were taking me, but the sea swallowed every word.

The deeper we swam, the colder it became. The current thinned until it felt like moving through glass. The glow of the surface disappeared completely, replaced by streaks of faint blue light running like veins through the rock. Pressure built around my ribs. My lungs burned. My thoughts began to fragment, slipping apart like sand between fingers.

Once or twice, I drifted toward the edge of consciousness, only to be jolted awake by flashes of movement—a torch burning with liquid fire, a cluster of eyes gleaming in the dark, the distant rumble of something vast shifting beneath the seabed. I remember the faint sound of chanting, low and rhythmic, not words but vibrations that rippled through the water like a heartbeat.

At some point, they passed through a gate: two towering slabs of volcanic glass etched with symbols that pulsed faintly as we approached. The instant we crossed between them, the pressure changed. The water felt denser, heavier, almost alive.

Through the haze, I glimpsed what looked like an entire world carved from the abyss. Pillars of black glass rose from the ocean floor, their tips crowned with glowing coral that bled light into the dark. Bridges arched between them, delicate and curved, and beneath those arches shimmered clusters of figures moving with quiet, deliberate grace. The sound of their tails slicing through the current was the only music.

We descended further, past tunnels lined with molten seams and hanging lanterns shaped like blooming shells. Every surface glowed faintly, the light reflecting in shifting patterns on the carriers' armor. They moved without words, without hesitation, like a single mind guiding many bodies.

I remember one last glimpse of the chasm below—a vast, jagged wound in the seafloor, breathing light with every pulse—and then the world narrowed to a single point of heat at the base of my skull. The glow around me blurred, twisting into streaks.

And then, nothing.

When I wake, the water tastes of ash and heat. My head throbs. The faint light flickering through the chamber walls paints everything in shades of obsidian and blue.

When I wake, the water tastes of ash and heat. My head throbs. The faint light flickering through the chamber walls paints everything in shades of obsidian and blue.

For a long time, I just float. I don't move, don't breathe too deeply—afraid the moment I do, the world will collapse again. The water here is still and thick, humming faintly against my skin. Each breath feels like it's coated in dust and minerals, raw and unfiltered, far from the sweet, processed currents of Lurea.

My body aches. My tail drags slightly, weighed down by fatigue. When I lift my hand, a faint shimmer of blue light trails from my fingertips before fading into the dark. I stare at it until the glow disappears.

They took me.
The realization settles like stone.

I'm not in the palace anymore. Not even close. The last thing I remember is the chaos, the whirlpool swallowing the Driftborn, Tarek's hand slipping from mine, the crest of the Drains flashing through the dark. Now—silence. No Council shouting. No bells. No distant hum of the city's Pulse. Only the muted breathing of a place that feels alive in a way I can't name.

I press a hand to my chest. The blue light beneath my skin pulses once, steady but faint. Still there. Still mine.

The thought doesn't comfort me.

I wonder if maybe they were right—if the sea really did reject me. Or maybe it just spit me out where I belong.

I push myself upright, tail brushing against the warm glass floor. The walls curve upward, etched with slow-moving light, like veins filled with molten current. The surface is rough in some places, polished in others, and when I press my palm against it, I feel a faint vibration running beneath, like the heartbeat of something immense and sleeping.

The light shifts in uneven waves, dimming and brightening, casting the room in different shades of blue and gold. My reflection stares back at me from the glass—hair tangled and wild, skin pale from exhaustion, eyes glowing faintly like dying embers.

I don't recognize her.

For a long moment, I just stare. The quiet swallows everything. My breathing. My fear. My thoughts.

What am I doing here? What do they want from me?

I think of my mother, her hands trembling as she tried to contain what she'd created. Of my father, choosing the kingdom over the child he swore to protect. Of Tarek, lost somewhere above. I think of the Council's word—*containment*—and realize how easily I might have traded one cage for another.

The ache behind my eyes sharpens. My throat tightens. The salt that burns my cheeks isn't from the sea.

"I didn't ask for this," I whisper into the water. My voice sounds small, swallowed almost instantly. "I didn't want any of it."

The blue veins in the wall pulse once in response, faint but clear. Like the sea heard me.

I curl my tail beneath me, pulling myself into a ball. The heat from the glass seeps through my skin, soothing and strange, as if the place itself is trying to calm me. I notice how steady the current is—no pull, no resistance. Just movement. Constant and alive.

It's almost peaceful.

I close my eyes, letting the warmth soak into me. The exhaustion that's been chasing me since the festival finally catches up, dragging me toward sleep.

But before I drift, a sound stirs in the distance—a low, resonant vibration that feels less like a noise and more like a calling. It comes from deep below, slow and deliberate, like a heartbeat echoing through the hollow walls.

I lift my head, listening. The rhythm is familiar. It's the same pulse that flared beneath my skin when the Heartwake touched me.

The water trembles, faintly, around me. I'm not sure if I'm afraid or in awe.

The floor beneath me isn't coral—it's smooth, black glass, warm to the touch, veined with glowing fissures that pulse faintly like veins of molten light. The room itself is carved into a dome of volcanic rock, the ceiling latticed with holes that breathe light from the ocean above. The air hums faintly, alive.

Movement catches my eye. A shape glides closer through the haze—a man, tall, his skin a deep bronze that shimmers like wet stone. His eyes are bright, the same impossible blue that once spilled from my veins. His tail is long and serrated, patterned with ash-gray markings that ripple with his every motion.

"Where—" My voice cracks. "Where am I?"

"The Hollow," he says, his tone deep, measured. "Home of the forgotten."

The Hollow. I've heard the name whispered like a curse. The Drains' refuge, carved into the volcanic scars of the lower sea—where no light from the upper currents reaches, where outcasts vanish and the sea's laws fail to bind.

I glance around. The city stretches far beyond the chamber's walls. I can see narrow bridges of black glass threading across vast chasms, homes carved into cliffs that glow faintly from within. Everything gleams—the kind of beauty born from ruin.

The man watches me carefully. "You're safe, Sparkblood."

The word chills me. "Don't call me that."

He tilts his head, amused. "It's not a name we fear here."

I study him. "Who are you?"

"Walder," he says simply. "Keeper of the Hollow, and now—keeper of you, it seems."

I shift, instinctively defensive. "If you plan to keep me here, you'll have to—"

He raises a hand. "Peace. We don't cage miracles."

I flinch at the word. "I'm not a miracle."

"Then what are you?"

I don't answer. Because I don't know anymore.

Walder's gaze softens. "You've seen what your kind call order. Their balance. Their Pulse. Tell me, did it ever feel alive to you?"

I shake my head. "It felt... still."

"Exactly." He gestures for me to follow. "Come. I want to show you something."

I hesitate, then push off from the floor. The current in here is strange—thick but gentle, like it's guiding rather than pushing. As we move, the corridors of the Hollow unfold around us. Columns of volcanic glass rise from the floor, each one carved with swirling symbols that glow from within. The air vibrates faintly, and I realize the sound is not silence but energy—steady, constant, breathing.

The further we go, the warmer it gets. The cracks in the walls widen, spilling molten light across the passage. The water thrums louder now, pressing against my skin until it feels like my heartbeat is syncing with something deep below.

Walder stops at the edge of a massive cavern.

The sight steals the breath from my lungs.

The floor drops away into a vast chasm, and at its center lies a wound in the earth—a jagged fissure stretching miles across, glowing with liquid light that pulses upward like the beat of a living heart. The water around it shimmers, tinted gold and blue, bending under the force of the energy it emits.

"The Heartwake," he says softly. "The sea's first breath. Where life began, and where it's beginning again."

I stare at it, transfixed. "It's beautiful."

"It's alive," he corrects. "And dying. The upper kingdom drains it for power. Your father's engineers built conduits that choke the sea's heart to keep their Pulse steady. They call us rebels for cutting the lines—but we're only clearing its veins."

I turn toward him. "You think destroying the Pulse will save the sea?"

"I think the Pulse already died when your people built it."

The words sting. "My people?"

“The Flowed. The Crown. The Council.” His eyes glint. “You come from the world that buried us. But you, Sparkblood... you’re not of it. You’re its answer.”

I shake my head. “I didn’t choose this.”

“No one chooses evolution.”

He moves closer, his voice lower now. “Do you know what Navedia’s rebellion was, truly? Not chaos. Not vengeance. It was the sea learning to change. The gods feared what we were becoming—so they named it heresy. They silenced the Spark, sealed the Heartwake, and told your kind it was divine punishment. But the sea never forgot. It waited for someone who could breathe both still water and storm.”

The glow from the fissure reflects in his eyes as he looks at me. “You.”

The words echo through me, both impossible and inevitable. The current swirls around my tail, tugging softly, like it agrees.

For a long time, neither of us speaks. I stare down into the Heartwake, the light shimmering across my skin, and for a moment it feels as though it’s staring back.

Somewhere above, the surface currents shift. I can feel it—a pull, a tremor, a heartbeat that isn’t mine. The water doesn’t feel cold. It feels like it’s *waiting*.

CHAPTER TEN

The Deep

Walder's chamber feels like the inside of a living storm.

The walls ripple faintly, streaked with molten light that twists and coils like veins of fire beneath glass. Every sound—the distant rush of the Heartwake below, the rhythmic breath of the Hollow itself—feels amplified here. The air tastes metallic, charged.

Walder waits at the far end of the room, framed by a pillar of glowing coral that spirals upward, its tips sparking faint threads of blue. His eyes catch the light as I approach, and for a moment they look almost inhuman—something born deeper than the rest of us.

"You've seen the Hollow," he says, voice low and patient. "You've seen what the sea has become under the Crown's rule. You know now what your kind has done to us."

"I'm not *my kind,*" I say quietly.

"No?" His gaze sharpens. "The blood in your veins says otherwise. Half Flowed. Half landborn. Daughter of a queen who tried to control the sea's heart."

I bite down on the edge of my tongue to keep from lashing back. "I didn't choose what I am."

"No one does," he agrees. "But you can choose what to do with it."

He gestures toward the glowing coral beside him. "The Pulse falters. The sea is bleeding from the inside, and your power—your Spark—is the only force left that can change it. Lead us, Maren of the Still Water. Help us take back what was stolen."

It takes me a second to process what he's asking. When I do, my chest goes cold.

"You want me to lead a war," I say flatly.

"I want you to *finish* one," Walder answers. "Navedia's rebellion began long before you were born. It ended when the Crown sealed us away and called it peace. But peace built on suffocation isn't peace—it's rot. You've seen it. The Council rules through fear of the sea, not faith in it."

"And you think a revolution will fix that?"

He steps closer, slow and deliberate. "I think the ocean is ready to breathe again. And it needs someone to show it how."

The weight of his words crushes the air between us. My fingers twitch with static, small threads of light sparking against my palms before fading.

"I don't want to fight anyone," I say. "I don't want to lead anyone. I just..." My voice catches. "I just want to *belong*."

He studies me for a long time, something unreadable flickering behind his eyes. "You will never belong to a world that fears you."

"Then I'll find one that doesn't."

The coral lights around us flare as if reacting to my voice, electricity skimming the surface of the glass. My pulse spikes; the glow under my skin ignites. "You think I want this? You think I asked to be a weapon?"

"Not a weapon," Walder says, unmoved. "A key."

The word snaps something in me. "Then you should've left me locked."

The current erupts before I can stop it. A wave of electricity bursts from my chest, flashing across the room in jagged lines. The coral pillars convulse, sending out showers of sparks. Walder doesn't move. He lets the storm roll past him until the last crackle fades.

Then he looks at me—not angry, not afraid, just calm in that impossible, infuriating way.

"You can fight me," he says, voice quiet now. "You can fight the sea. But you can't fight what you are."

"I don't want your cause," I whisper. "I just want to live."

"And living is exactly what they won't let you do."

Before I can answer, something cold presses against my neck—a sting, a pulse. I turn, but the world tilts too quickly. The Drains behind me lower their hands, the injection tubes glinting faintly in the dim light.

My vision fractures. The room blurs into waves of blue and gold. Walder's face swims in front of me, a shadow against fire. "Rest," he says. "When you wake, the sea will still need you."

Then the dark swallows me whole.

It isn't just the absence of light—it's absolute, endless. A darkness that feels alive, folding inward like deep water closing over a sinking ship. For a while, there's no pain, no sound, no body—just the soft pulse of something vast and unseen. I can't tell if I'm dreaming, drowning, or dissolving.

Then, slowly, light begins to bloom.

Not the blue of the Heartwake, not the molten shimmer of volcanic glass—but something softer. It grows beneath me, spreading upward through the dark like dawn through mist. My body floats toward it, weightless.

The light sharpens, and suddenly I'm rising—not swimming, not being carried, but rising *through* the water, through the cold and pressure and silence, until the darkness thins into gray. A surface forms above me, rippling faintly like glass.

I break through it.

The world explodes into color.

For a heartbeat, I can't breathe. The air slams into my lungs—sweet, sharp, impossibly dry—and it *burns*. I cough, gasping, but the pain fades quickly, replaced by an ache of wonder. The sky stretches forever, vast and open, painted with the colors of dusk. Clouds drift like slow creatures. Light spills across the waves, touching my skin with gold.

I reach for the water, but it's different now—light, playful, frothing against my fingertips. My hair clings to my face, heavy with salt. The air hums with sounds

I've never known: gull cries, the rhythmic crash of waves, wind rustling through unseen things.

And then I realize I'm not floating anymore.

I'm *lying* on something solid—something that doesn't move with the tide. My body feels strange, unbalanced. The weight distribution is wrong. I glance down and freeze.

Where my tail should be, there are legs.

Two limbs, pale and trembling, bent at odd angles, ending in shapes that fan out into smaller, jointed fins—no, not fins. *Feet.*

I stare, transfixed. The surface of my skin glows faintly, reflecting sunlight like wet glass. When I shift, the muscles respond in strange, independent ways—flexing, curling, anchoring.

For a moment, panic flashes through me. My first instinct is to dive back under, to hide the wrongness. But when I move, the sand beneath me shifts—soft and warm and alive. The feeling roots me in place.

I drag a hand across the surface, leaving shallow grooves. The grains glitter in the light like powdered coral. The water licks at the edges of my new limbs, cool and teasing. I should feel fear. Instead, I feel something like awe.

The world above the sea is nothing like I imagined. It's louder, harsher, unfiltered—but breathtaking. Every movement of the wind against my skin feels electric, every sound so crisp it might shatter.

I lift one leg carefully, watching how the muscles tighten and release. The limb trembles, heavy and foreign, but alive. The concept of balance, of *standing,* flits through my mind, strange and tantalizing. I plant both hands in the sand, try to rise.

The first attempt sends me collapsing forward. The second gets me halfway. The third—by some miracle—lifts me upright.

I sway, unsteady. The wind brushes against me, cold against the salt drying on my skin. For a moment, I am both creature and question—neither sea nor sky.

I take one hesitant step toward the water, legs buckling, but I catch myself. The sea stretches before me, glittering with sunlight, endless and familiar yet impossibly far away.

A feeling unfurls inside me—half wonder, half ache.

If I can stand here, breathe this air, touch both worlds... what else have I been told is impossible?

The wind answers, soft and hollow, and the light begins to fade. The edges of the world blur, the horizon tilts, and the colors bleed back into darkness. The surface collapses into reflection, and then the sea reclaims me.

When I wake again, it's to warmth. Not the suffocating heat of volcanic glass, but the clean warmth of current flow wrapping around my tail like a gentle tether. My head pounds, but my body feels light—too light. The faint glow beneath my skin pulses in time with the slow throb of the Hollow.

I'm not in the chamber anymore. I'm in a circular pool surrounded by coral vines that hum faintly with energy. The air hums, thick with ozone and salt.

A voice drifts from above. "Easy there, Sparkblood. Don't fight it."

It's not Walder—it's a woman this time, her hair a halo of pale strands floating around her face, her eyes the same eerie blue as the fissures below. She offers a hand, steady and sure. "Breathe with it," she says. "The current doesn't want to hurt you. It just wants to move through you."

"I didn't agree to this," I murmur, but the words sound far away, pulled apart by the flow.

"No one does," she says gently. "That's how the sea chooses."

She guides my hand toward a coral structure beside the pool. It's dormant, colorless—just fossilized shell. "Channel your energy into this," she says. "Don't force it. Let it rise when you breathe."

I hesitate. "What happens if I can't control it?"

"Then it controls you."

The blue light flares beneath my skin before I can stop it. I exhale, and the current answers. Lightning arcs from my palm, threading through the coral in shimmering webs. The dead reef glows, light spilling from its cracks until it blooms again—color racing through it like veins finding blood. The vibration it sends back through the water is subtle but alive, like the reef itself just remembered how to exist.

I gasp and pull back, but the woman smiles. "Good. You're learning."

Days blur into days. I don't see Walder often—only the echoes of his orders, carried by whispers in the current. They're training me, though they don't call it that. They teach me to channel electricity through coral conduits, to wake dormant reefs, to sense the sea's weak spots—the Pulse distortions left behind by the Council's conduits. The Hollow vibrates with their energy, a city of whispers and resistance, half sacred and half rebellion.

Every time I use my power, it feels easier. The lightning that once burned now hums through me like blood. When I close my eyes, I can sense the distortions stretching through the ocean—threads of tension waiting to snap. I should feel stronger, but every new surge leaves me emptier.

Sometimes, late in the cycle when the sea goes quiet, I think about Tarek. About my mother, trapped somewhere above. About the city that was once my home.

I tell myself I'm just learning to survive. But each day I stay here, the word *Sparkblood* feels less like a curse and more like a command.

And when Walder finally returns, standing at the edge of the training pool with light from the Heartwake burning behind him, I realize the truth I've been avoiding:

I'm no longer running from the sea. The sea is running *through me.*

CHAPTER ELEVEN

The Brother

The Hollow quivers before I even hear the alarm.

At first, it's faint—like a shift in the water's pulse, a subtle tightening around the chest. Then it grows sharper, heavier. The Heartwake's glow wavers across the obsidian walls, colors splintering into uneasy flashes of gold and blue.

Something's wrong.

I can *feel* it. The current isn't breathing right—it's folding, bending around something it doesn't want.

Walder rises from his seat, face unreadable. "Someone's entered the Trench."

The murmurs that follow sound distant. The words blur. All I hear is the ocean itself, whispering my name through the current. A ripple of familiarity rides the pull—frantic, reckless, and unmistakably young.

“Stay here,” Walder orders, but his voice is already fading behind me.

Because I know that pulse.

Zeke.

The name pierces the water like a blade, slicing through the haze of my thoughts. It echoes somewhere deep inside me—too familiar, too alive to be imagined. For a moment, I can’t move. My body just hovers in the dim light of the Hollow, every nerve on edge, listening.

Then I feel it again—*him*.

A vibration against the current, faint but distinct, the way I used to recognize the beat of his tail as a child when he’d try to sneak up on me during training. It’s faster now, more erratic, pulsing with heat and conviction. No one else moves like that.

“Zeke,” I whisper, and the sea answers with a low, mournful tremor.

Images flood my mind—him laughing as bubbles burst from his nose, chasing after my shadow in the coral fields; the way he used to beg to train beside me, even when his hands blistered from the current staff. The memory burns, colliding with the sharp image of him standing in the throne room the day I was condemned. The way he looked at me—not with fear, but disbelief.

He’s coming. I don’t need Walder to confirm it; I can *feel* him. His current is too bright, too loud, the way only palace-trained swimmers move—disciplined, precise, but still pulsing with that adolescent defiance he’s never learned to hide.

I can’t decide if the feeling rising in my chest is terror or love.

The sea around me tightens, trembling against my skin like it senses my hesitation. Walder's voice drifts faintly from somewhere behind me, warning me to stay, to let the currents do what they must—but I'm already moving.

The Hollow's light fades behind me as I swim into the corridor tunnels that wind upward toward the trench's mouth. The water grows cooler, sharper, filled with mineral ash that burns the lungs when you breathe too fast. My heartbeat quickens.

The tunnel narrows, the walls sweating faint light from veins of glowing glass. I brush my hand along one as I pass; the surface vibrates faintly, as if the sea itself is whispering a warning through the stone.

Zeke's pulse grows stronger. The rhythm of it builds beneath my ribs until it almost matches my own—two currents converging, identical yet oppositional. It's like being pulled toward a storm.

By the time I emerge from the tunnel into open water, the world feels different. The Hollow's warmth is gone, replaced by the cold stretch of the lower sea.

The current here pulls unevenly, as though the ocean itself can't decide which way to move. The taste of iron fills my mouth, heavy and old. I glance upward, where faint trails of light shimmer like dying stars through the gloom, marking the descent of something foreign.

Soldiers.

The water distorts with the pulse of their current fields—controlled, synchronized. Their armor glints dully as they cut through the deep, each movement too uniform to be anything but royal-trained. And in front of them, blazing like a young sun, swims Zeke.

The golden arcs of his current burn against the dark, molten and bright, rippling through the trench like wildfire. He doesn't hesitate, doesn't falter. He's following something—*someone.*

Me.

The currents tighten the further I swim from the Hollow, pulling like threads caught on hooks. The light dims, bleeding into murky blue. By the time I reach the outer ridge of the Trench, the world feels smaller—like the sea itself is holding its breath.

I see them before I hear them: flashes of gold, the disciplined rhythm of formation. Palace soldiers. And at the center of their ranks—Zeke.

He's grown. Taller, sharper around the edges, his once-boyish face hardened by determination. But the glow that flickers across his body is still familiar—bright, golden-orange, his current burning through the water in clean arcs that crackle against the dark.

"Tarek," I whisper.

He's already there, hovering between them and the drop, his presence like an anchor. The light of his current is different from Zeke's—deep bronze streaked with silver, thrumming in measured waves that pulse along his arms. It moves like tempered lightning, strong but patient.

Zeke spots him and signals his guards to hold position. "Step aside," he says, his voice distorted through the press of the sea.

Tarek's tone is calm, but the current around him coils in warning. "You shouldn't be here."

Zeke's reply cuts through the water like glass. "Neither should she."

The soldiers behind him shift uneasily. They're trained for combat, but not for *this*. The Trench hums with a strange power—one that doesn't belong to them.

"I said step aside," Zeke repeats, and this time the command carries weight.

Tarek doesn't move. "If you want her, you'll have to go through me."

The water stills between them, just long enough for the light from the Heartwake to catch on their faces. Then Zeke lunges.

The impact sends a shockwave through the trench. Zeke's current bursts outward in ribbons of gold, spiraling through the dark like molten sunfire. Tarek meets him mid-strike, and the collision lights the water. Sparks tear free, scattering like stars.

Their movements blur—Zeke's precision against Tarek's power. Zeke fights like someone who's been drilled for years—tight form, quick strikes, never wasting motion. Every arc of his blade leaves trails of light that burn and fade behind him.

Tarek absorbs, redirects. His current thrums low and steady, more a vibration than a flash. It ripples through his body, building momentum before exploding in sudden bursts that send Zeke spinning backward.

Zeke recovers fast, flipping his tail and sending a blast of compressed current toward Tarek. The water screams under the force. For a moment, it feels like he might actually overpower him. The boy I remember—the one who used to chase glowfish through the palace corridors—is gone. In his place is something fierce, unrelenting.

"Stop this!" I shout, but the sea swallows my voice.

Tarek deflects another strike, barely. "You've gotten stronger," he says between breaths, eyes narrowing.

"I had to," Zeke snaps, his voice cracking—not from weakness, but emotion. "You think you're the only one who trained for something? The only one who lost her?"

"She's not yours to lose."

"She's my *sister!*" The golden light around Zeke flares so bright it blinds me. The current surges, and for an instant, I see him as he's always wanted to be—brave, brilliant, unstoppable.

But Tarek is older. Wiser. His strength doesn't burn—it builds.

He waits for the right moment, lets Zeke's fury crest, and then—moves.

His hand closes around the younger boy's wrist. The bronze light in his veins flashes white, and the currents between them buckle. Zeke's blade spins free, tumbling into the dark below. The light around him sputters, dimming to a dull gold.

They both freeze, breathing hard. The air between them hums with leftover static.

Tarek's voice is quiet when he finally speaks. "You fight well, Zeke. But this isn't the way."

Zeke glares at him, trembling. "You don't understand," he says. "They'll declare rebellion if she doesn't come back. They'll hunt her. They'll kill Mother."

The words sink like stones. The fury drains from his voice, leaving something fragile beneath it.

"I can't let her drown down here," he whispers. "Not again."

Tarek's grip softens, but he doesn't let go. "She's not drowning," he says. "She's breathing for the first time."

Zeke jerks free, tail curling tight beneath him. His light flickers uncertainly. He's shaking—half from exhaustion, half from something deeper.

"She belongs with us," he says. "With *me*."

Tarek studies him, then glances over his shoulder—straight toward where I'm hiding among the coral ridges. For a moment, his eyes meet mine.

He knows I've been watching.

"Go back," he tells Zeke. "Tell your father you found nothing. Tell him the sea claimed her. It's the only way to save her."

Zeke's mouth opens, but no sound comes. His tail lashes once, golden scales scattering light into the dark. Then he looks toward the trench below, toward the unseen glow of the Heartwake, and his voice trembles when he speaks again.

"I'll find her," he says. "Even if it means following her into the dark."

He signals his soldiers, and the group begins to retreat—slowly, reluctantly, the gold fading into the distance until the dark swallows it.

Tarek doesn't move until the last flicker of their light is gone. Only then does he turn toward me. His expression is unreadable.

"He's not done," he says quietly. "He won't stop."

I nod, though my chest aches. "He's just a boy."

"You were just a girl," Tarek says. "Before the sea decided otherwise."

The words hit harder than he means them to. Maybe because I can still hear the edge of pity in them—or maybe because they're true. I don't feel like that girl anymore. The one who believed the sea was kind, who thought her family could hold her above the tide if she just tried hard enough.

I look toward the dark where Zeke vanished, the faint golden echo of his current already fading into the abyss. The silence that follows feels enormous. It's as if the water itself is waiting for me to choose something.

My fingers curl against the rock wall, and the texture bites back—rough, real. I stare at it until the ache in my chest steadies. "He shouldn't have come," I say finally.

Tarek exhales through his nose, but doesn't reply.

"He doesn't belong here."

"Neither do you," he says, gently but not unkindly.

I flinch, because it's not an accusation. It's a truth I can't ignore.

The currents around us have gone still, eerily still. The trench wall hums faintly beneath my hand, carrying the echo of the Heartwake far below. I can feel its pulse—slow, deliberate, as if the sea itself is considering what's just happened.

"I should go home," I murmur, the words tasting wrong even as I say them. "If Zeke found me, others will too. They'll think the Drains took me prisoner. They'll send more soldiers. Maybe my father himself. If I go back now—"

"They'll put you in the Vault," Tarek interrupts.

His tone is flat, but the image flashes behind my eyes anyway: the Vault's iron gates, the whisper of pressure seals closing, the kind of silence that doesn't end.

I turn away, trying to push the thought down. "They wouldn't—"

"They would. You know they would. You saw what they did to your mother for less."

I want to argue, to defend him—my father, my kingdom—but the words never come. The memory of the council chamber crashes over me again: the faces of the nobles twisting with fear, the sound of them deciding what I was instead of who. The look in his eyes as he let them.

Zeke showing up means they haven't stopped looking. They're desperate enough to risk the Trench, desperate enough to send a child into the dark. Which means Walder is right—the Council isn't afraid of rebellion anymore. They're preparing for it.

A dull ache starts behind my ribs, spreading outward. "If they declare war..."

Tarek's hand brushes mine, grounding. "They already have. They just haven't said it out loud yet."

The current shivers between us, sending tiny sparks of static through the water. I can see the faint bronze glow of his current flaring around his arms, pulsing in time with my own blue light. The difference between us—his calm control, my restless electricity—feels sharper than ever.

"I don't want to fight," I whisper.

He looks at me then, really looks at me, and there's something like sorrow behind his steady gaze. "No one does, Maren. Not at first."

I let the silence swallow us again. The Heartwake pulses below, faint but persistent, beating like something alive. I can almost feel it inside me now, mirroring my own heartbeat.

"I don't know how long it's been," I admit. "Days? Weeks? The light doesn't change down here. Everything feels... endless."

"Long enough for the world above to start shaking," he says. "Long enough for the sea to notice what you are."

I close my eyes. The water tastes different—bitter, briny, alive. Somewhere far above, Lurea still gleams with its artificial light, pretending the ocean is tame. My brother is probably swimming home now, carrying stories of monsters and rebellion. My father is sitting on his throne, telling himself he did everything he could.

And here I am, caught between them and the depths.

When I open my eyes, Tarek is watching me carefully, but he doesn't say anything. Maybe he sees it already—the shift in my posture, the way my tail has stilled.

Half of me wants to swim upward, to break through the layers of pressure and light until I see home again. I imagine bursting through the palace gates, grabbing Zeke's hand, shouting sense into the King until he listens.

But the other half knows better.

If I return now, I'll be caged before I can speak. My current will be studied, dissected, harnessed. They'll call it protection, but it'll be punishment—the quiet kind that looks like mercy until you can't breathe anymore.

And somewhere beneath that fear, another truth coils tighter: if the Council is truly preparing for war, then the Hollow won't survive without me.

I float there, staring into the endless dark, feeling the weight of both worlds pressing on my chest.

Finally, I whisper, "He found me because I still belong to them. But I think the sea's trying to tell me I belong somewhere else now."

Tarek nods once, slow. "Then listen to it."

The light from the Heartwake rises faintly through the water, brushing against my skin in waves of blue and gold. For a moment, it feels like the sea itself is exhaling—like it's waiting for my answer.

CHAPTER TWELVE

The Message

I wake to silence, the kind that feels heavy enough to press against bone.

The Hollow is never truly quiet—there's always the murmur of the sea, the slow heartbeat of the Heartwake thrumming beneath—but this is different. This silence *waits*.

The light is strange too. Pale, fractured. It filters through the walls in slow-moving ribbons, shimmering like ghost water. I push myself upright, every movement slow, the aftertaste of sleep still clinging to me like salt.

Something glows near the far end of the chamber.

At first, I think it's a lantern someone forgot to extinguish. Then it moves—drifting toward me, round and smooth, reflecting the molten glow from below. A sphere of glass, the size of my hand, gliding through the water as though following the sound of my pulse.

I reach for it, hesitating only a moment. The surface hums faintly when my fingers brush it, the same vibration I feel when I touch the coral conduits in the training hall.

The sphere splits softly down its center, releasing a slow shimmer of light.

And then I hear her.

"Mar—" My mother's voice catches, trembles. "Maren, if you're hearing this... then the sea has already done what I feared most."

My breath falters. The chamber fades away. It's just her voice now—clear and impossibly near.

"They've imprisoned me. Treason, they're calling it. For what I did to save you."

I sink lower, my tail curling beneath me. The edges of the room blur.

"I wanted to wait, to tell you everything when I could see your face," she continues. "But Zeke came to me, and I knew I couldn't. He told me where to find you—he said the Drains would protect you. I think he was right."

Her voice breaks slightly on his name. She sounds small, like the weight of the ocean is finally too much for her lungs to bear.

"There's something I never told you. Something I thought I could protect you from by hiding it."

The sphere flickers, and suddenly her image blooms inside it—her hair loose, eyes shadowed, the faint glow of her coral lungs pulsing through her skin. Behind her, I can see the faint silhouette of the Vault's chamber walls, their sharp symmetry unmistakable.

"When I underwent the Rite of Binding," she says, "I thought I understood what it meant. I thought binding coral to my lungs would only let me breathe the sea. I didn't realize it would *change* me."

Her hands rise to her chest, fingers splayed over the faint, pink light pulsing beneath her collarbone. "The coral isn't inert, Maren. It grows. It *remembers*. And when I carried you, it wove itself into your heart before I ever knew it could."

The words ripple through me like a tide.

"The spark you carry—it isn't a gift from the gods or a curse of rebellion. It's fusion. The coral's energy met the Pulse inside me, but it didn't stop there. It found something else. Something *human*."

I don't breathe.

"The sea's power and human energy don't belong together," she whispers, as if afraid the walls might be listening. "But you... you made them belong. You were never meant to destroy the Pulse, Maren. You *are* the bridge between what lives above and what breathes below."

I press my hand to my chest, to the faint blue light beneath my skin, feeling it thrum in response.

Selara's reflection in the sphere smiles faintly, though her eyes are full of tears. "I thought I could teach you to hide it. That if you never used it, the sea would forget. But I see now—it was never meant to sleep."

She reaches forward, palm open, as if she could touch me through the water. "You are my greatest mistake and my greatest creation. If the sea chose you, then maybe it's finally ready to change."

The image flickers, distorts. A voice shouts somewhere beyond her—a guard, harsh and metallic. She glances back, her face tightening, then turns again to the sphere.

"Zeke loves you," she says quickly. "He doesn't understand what you are yet, but he will. I only ask that when you see him again, you don't hate him for the chains he's been taught to wear."

The sound of metal striking coral rings through the water. She gasps, clutching the sphere in her hands.

"Don't let them tell your story for you, Maren." Her voice trembles now, but her eyes are steady. "Whatever happens to me, remember—your heart isn't a weapon. It's a map."

The image fractures. Light bursts outward like shattered glass, and then the sphere collapses inward, dissolving into a cloud of glowing dust that drifts toward me. I reach out, and it settles gently into my palm, sinking into my skin like salt melting in water.

For a long time, I can't move. The sea is too still, the weight of her words too much to hold.

Fusion. Not magic. Not prophecy. Just... creation.

The coral's rhythm. My heartbeat. The Pulse. All of it woven into one impossible thread.

I close my eyes, pressing both hands against my chest. The current there hums faintly, alive, constant.

The world above thinks they can divide the sea from the sky. My mother thought she could divide her heart from mine.

None of them could.

The light fades gradually, like the sea is exhaling after holding its breath too long. Tiny bubbles rise from the floor and cling to my arms, soft as whispers. For a while, I just float there, the silence around me no longer heavy, but steady—almost tender.

The message has left something behind, a warmth that lingers where the sphere dissolved, as if her touch is still imprinted on the current. I let it settle into me. The ache in my chest eases, the pulse beneath my skin slows.

Outside my chamber, the Hollow stirs. The great city beneath the sea is never fully asleep; even in its quiet moments, the water hums with movement. Faint streams of molten light pulse through the glass veins of the walls, like distant veins of lightning. The glow ripples outward, painting the ridges of my palms in soft blue and gold.

I press my forehead against the glass, closing my eyes. The water feels warmer than it should—alive.

Mother's voice still echoes inside me, wrapping itself around my heart: *You're not a curse. You're a bridge.*

I whisper her words back into the sea, testing them on my tongue, and the sound is steadier than I expect.

Outside, I can see the faint outlines of the Drains drifting through the trench, their light patterns bright and purposeful. They move like a heartbeat—collective, sure, unafraid of the dark. There's something strangely peaceful about it. The ocean is wide enough to hold both ruin and beauty at once, and somehow, I fit into both.

Tarek finds me there, leaning against the glass wall. He doesn't say anything right away; he just watches the way the light plays against the water.

“I heard the Heartwake flare,” he says finally, voice low. “Did something happen?”

I nod, my throat still thick. “My mother.”

His eyes soften. “She found a way to reach you.”

“She told me the truth,” I say quietly. “About… what I am.”

He waits, but doesn’t press. Maybe he knows I’m not ready to say more.

For a long while, we just drift together, listening to the Hollow’s slow rhythm. There’s comfort in the quiet between us. Tarek’s presence has always been like that—a steady anchor in the pull of everything else.

“She’s brave,” he says finally.

“She’s trapped,” I answer.

He shakes his head. “Sometimes those are the same thing.”

A small smile tugs at my mouth before I can stop it. “You always make things sound like they’re supposed to make sense.”

“They usually do,” he says, a little grin flickering across his face. “Just not right away.”

The warmth of his current brushes against mine—a faint bronze shimmer curling around the blue beneath my skin. I let it happen, let the contact ease the tension that’s been coiled in me for too long.

“I think,” I murmur, “I finally understand why the sea wouldn’t let me die that day in the lab.”

Tarek looks at me, searching my face.

“It wasn’t saving me,” I say. “It was waiting for me to wake up.”

He tilts his head, thoughtful. “And now?”

“Now I’m listening.”

The Hollow hums softly in response, a deep, resonant sound that vibrates through the water. It feels almost like the sea approving.

I take a deep breath without feeling like I’m stealing air that doesn’t belong to me. The ache behind my ribs is still there, but it’s quieter now—less wound, more reminder.

I glance at Tarek. “Whatever comes next... I think I’m ready to stop running.”

He nods, slow and sure. “Then you’re already ahead of most.”

I close my eyes and let the warmth move through me, through everything. The sea doesn’t feel like it’s waiting to take something from me. It feels like it’s offering something back.

CHAPTER THIRTEEN
The Rising

The sea begins to shake before dawn.

It starts with a shiver that runs through the walls of the Hollow, small enough that most mistake it for current drift. But then the tremor grows, vibrating through the volcanic glass, humming against every bone in my body. The light veins in the floor flicker—blue, then gold, then blue again—out of sync with the Heartwake's usual rhythm.

I press my palm to the wall. The pulse that answers isn't steady anymore. It stutters like a frightened heart.

Outside my chamber, the Hollow wakes in motion. Drains dart through the corridors, their light patterns sharp and urgent. The current buzzes with tension, carrying the sound of shouted orders and metal scraping against stone. When I swim out, the water feels different—thicker, charged, alive with static.

"Tarek?"

He meets me halfway down the passage, his tail lashing to steady himself against another tremor. "You feel it too," he says. "It's not just here. The sensors are lighting up all the way to the outer ridge. Something's wrong with the Heartwake."

Before I can answer, a low rumble ripples through the trench. The lights dim, then flare again, flooding the corridor in molten gold. I clutch the nearest wall, heart pounding as the current shifts beneath us.

"What's happening?"

He shakes his head. "It's surging. Like it's trying to draw power from somewhere." His eyes flick to me—just for a heartbeat, but enough.

"Don't," I say. "It's not me."

But even as I speak, the water around us brightens, laced with thin ribbons of light that twist through the current like veins of lightning. They pulse in rhythm with my heartbeat.

Tarek sees it too. His jaw tightens. "We should find Walder."

The next tremor hits before I can answer. The entire corridor convulses, sending a shockwave through the glass floor that ripples up my tail. The veins of light in the walls flare—bright blue, then orange, then back to blue—as though the Hollow itself can't decide what pulse to follow.

We push forward, fighting the shifting current. It's stronger now, unpredictable, pulling and twisting in alternating bursts that make it hard to swim straight. A low sound rolls through the deep—a groan that seems to come from the trench itself. Dust and fragments of coral shake loose from the ceiling, drifting like ash through the water.

I glance toward the outer wall. Through the glass, the sea is alive with movement. Shadows of enormous creatures twist in the distance—sleek bodies gliding upward, drawn by something I can't see but can *feel*. The light from their bodies flickers faintly, a strange, luminous migration that sends a chill through me.

"They shouldn't be this close," I murmur. "They never come near the Hollow."

"They're following the current," Tarek says. "Or something in it."

Something in *me*.

I can feel the water responding again, the faint charge crawling across my skin, the hum of energy gathering around my ribs. The more I try to contain it, the louder it becomes.

By the time we reach the upper corridor, the glow of the Heartwake is visible even from here—a trembling gold that stains the water. Drains rush past us, shouting orders, their tails cutting streaks through the rising silt. One of them nearly collides with me, her eyes wide with panic.

"It's rising!" she gasps. "The Heartwake's rising!"

Tarek grabs her arm. "Where's Walder?"

"Council hall," she says, already pushing away. "He called everyone there. Says the sea's sending us a sign."

We exchange a glance. Neither of us says what we're thinking: Walder will see this chaos as prophecy, not warning.

The pressure grows heavier as we ascend, the water thick with warmth. Every pulse of the Heartwake beats through the Hollow's foundation, vibrating against my bones. The closer we get, the harder it is to tell if the current is shaking me, or if it's the other way around.

When we reach the main hall, the corridors are lit like sunrise—ribbons of molten light swirling through the glass columns, painting everything in shades of gold and crimson. The sound of the Heartwake is everywhere now, not just a hum but a steady, thunderous pulse that seems to match the rhythm of my heartbeat.

We round the final corner—and the full scope of it unfolds before me.

The council chamber of the Hollow burns with restless light. The Heartwake's glow filters through the floor in waves, painting every face in shifting colors. Drains line the perimeter, their armor glinting as they struggle to steady themselves against the tremors. Walder stands at the center, his expression sharpened by awe.

"Do you see it?" he says when we enter. "The sea itself is answering. The creatures of the deep are rising. The old currents are waking."

I follow his gaze to the far wall. Through the glass, I can see it—vast shapes moving in the dark. Leviathans. Winged rays larger than ships. Schools of glowing fish that have never come this high, their light spilling upward like a reversed waterfall. The sight is hauntingly beautiful. Terrifying.

"They're migrating," I whisper. "They shouldn't be here."

"They're coming home," Walder says, his voice thick with reverence. "This is the sign we've been waiting for. The Heartwake is calling the sea back to itself. The Flowed will choke on their own still water."

I shake my head. "No. You don't understand. This isn't balance—it's panic. The ocean's pulse is breaking."

He looks at me with something like pity. "You don't hear it, do you? The song beneath the chaos. The sea is *singing*through you, Maren. You are the proof of its will."

"Will?" I echo, my voice sharper than I intend. "You mean destruction."

He steps closer, lowering his voice. "For something new to live, the old must die. You know this."

"I know what it looks like when people call ruin rebirth."

The room trembles again. Dust spirals upward in shimmering clouds. I can feel the water vibrating under my skin, my current flaring without permission. It wants something. Not destruction—but connection. Completion.

"Walder, stop this," I plead. "If you rise now, you'll bring the whole sea down with you."

He studies me, his expression unreadable. "You've been touched by the Heartwake, but you still think like a Crown child. You still fear what you are."

"I'm not afraid," I say. But the tremor in my voice betrays me.

His smile is faint, almost kind. "Then prove it."

He turns to the gathered Drains. "Sound the call. The time has come. The Flowed have bled the sea dry long enough."

"No!"

The word bursts from me before I can think. Lightning flares from my skin, sharp and bright, striking the floor in a flash of blue. The shockwave ripples through the chamber, silencing everything. For a moment, no one moves.

Then the water shifts again—not from me this time, but from deep below. A surge rises from the trench, vast and violent, shaking the Hollow to its core. The walls groan. Light fractures into shards.

And then I *hear it*.

Not the Pulse. Not my own heartbeat. Something older. A voice—low, resonant, echoing through the current like a memory that never died.

Maren.

The word vibrates through me, through the Hollow, through the sea itself. Pressing against the edges of my mind.

Maren, child of the divided blood. Come home.

I stagger backward, clutching my head. Images flash behind my eyes—a face I've never seen, eyes like molten light, hands weaving through currents of fire and gold. A woman's silhouette framed by storm.

"Navedia," I breathe.

The name feels like it belongs to the water itself.

Her voice floods through me. *They silenced me once. They will not silence us again.*

Us.

I shake my head, forcing the word away. "You're not real. You're a myth. You're—"

But she laughs, soft and knowing. *My body died. My mind remained. The Heartwake remembers what the sea cannot bear to forget. You are its continuation. Its voice reborn.*

The light around me burns brighter, wrapping my arms, my chest, my throat. The currents hum with impossible energy, pressing outward, begging to be released.

Tarek's voice cuts through it. "Maren, breathe! Stay with me!"

I can barely hear him. The water sings, Navedia's voice entwined with mine. It feels like drowning and becoming all at once.

Let go, she whispers. *We can finish what they started.*

I fight it. I push back. "No. I'm not your weapon."

You're not. You're evolution.

The Heartwake surges again, a deep boom that shudders through the Hollow, scattering coral and glass. The light in my veins bursts outward, illuminating the entire chamber. I see the faces of the Drains turned upward, eyes wide with awe.

Walder drops to one knee, his voice reverent. "The Sparkblood has awakened."

As the sea roars around me, alive with rebellion and rising creatures, I realize I've already lost control. My pulse and the Heartwake's are one, and Navedia is still inside.

CHAPTER FOURTEEN

The Shattering

The ocean goes to war.

It begins as a sound—distant, low, like thunder trapped beneath miles of pressure. The tremors roll through the Hollow, rattling coral spires and shattering lanterns suspended from their chains. Every heartbeat hums with the same note, vibrating through the marrow of the sea itself.

The war drums of the deep.

From my vantage point at the upper ridge, I see it all unfolding below. The trench glows in pulses of blue and gold, the water illuminated by thousands of bodies moving in coordinated chaos. The Drains have risen.

Their currents flare across the battlefield like living fire—each one unique. I can see the signatures now: crimson streaks of thermal flame from the forge clans, pale ribbons of healing coral mist from the Lifebinders, sharp violet flashes of pressure burst from the

Trenchborn sentinels. Their energy intertwines, forming vast, luminous patterns across the dark.

And descending from the upper currents—Lurea's army.

The Flowed come in formation, columns of bright gold and steel slicing through the water, armor gleaming under the faint glow of current seals. The King's sigil burns on their chests, pulsing in perfect rhythm with the central Pulse towers that sustain their power. Behind them trail massive conduits that hum with contained pressure—cannons designed to fracture coral walls and collapse trenches.

Between them, the Heartwake burns—its glow visible even through the chaos. Every surge of power from the fissure sends a ring of molten light racing through the deep, shaking the currents into violent spirals.

I hover near the edge, the current around me trembling with every heartbeat.

They shouldn't have come.

Walder floats at the forefront of the Drains' formation, his body haloed by a mantle of white flame—his current alive, brilliant, beautiful. He raises his hand, and the sea obeys. The trench walls tremble as ancient coral roots stir awake, twisting upward like skeletal vines. The soldiers of Lurea brace against the pressure, their shields flaring in response, sending out golden barriers of energy that crackle where they meet Walder's surge.

The water between them ignites.

Currents collide, forming whirlpools that spiral into the abyss. Pressure bursts erupt like underwater explosions, distorting light and sound. Shards of coral spin through the dark, glittering like glass.

Then the first bodies fall—dragged into the trench by the shifting currents.

The sea screams.

It's not a sound the ear can hold—it's vibration and pressure, a thousand frequencies colliding at once until the water itself seems to tear apart. The shockwave punches through me, crushing and hollow, knocking every breath from my lungs.

Currents spiral in every direction. The light fractures. Bodies and debris twist together in the torrent. The metallic taste of blood and ash floods the water, stinging my tongue.

A burst of gold flashes past—palace soldiers scattering through the surge. Their current fields shimmer, failing under the strain. The Drains respond in kind, their light colder, wilder—like lightning dragged through deep water. The two collide, a swirl of power so bright it feels like standing inside a star.

Above, the coral towers of the Hollow groan under the weight of the chaos. Fractures race along their surfaces, spilling filaments of molten blue. A current cannon fires from the Lurean line, the recoil echoing through the sea like thunder. The projectile doesn't just tear through coral—it *implodes* it, sucking the light inward before bursting it back out in a bloom of bubbles and shards.

I duck behind a jut of broken ridge as the force ripples past. The pressure hits like a slap, flattening me against the stone. My body burns with the electric residue of my own power—uninvited, uncontrolled.

The blue veins under my skin glow faintly, reacting to every surge.

Somewhere ahead, Walder's voice carries through the din—a deep, commanding resonance that bends the current around him. His soldiers answer, their lights converging into a single spiral formation that pushes forward through the turbulence. The Flowed respond in perfect synchrony, shields rising, tridents crackling with compressed current energy.

The world narrows to light and movement. Every flash blinds. Every pulse rattles the bones. The Hollow's song—once slow and sacred—has become a storm.

I try to swim forward, but the current slams me back. My gills burn. The water tastes of oil and iron. All around me, the war churns on—a terrible ballet of color and motion.

A Drains fighter spins past me, his armor cracked, eyes glassy. Another—a woman I'd trained with just days ago—throws out her hand, summoning a burst of heat that melts a Flowed blade mid-strike. The temperature spike sears my skin as it rushes by.

The deeper I push into the trench, the worse it gets. The Heartwake's light has gone wild, surging upward in erratic bursts that bend the currents. Pressure waves collide, creating pockets where the water turns strangely thin, and every breath feels like drowning.

And then I see him—Tarek.

He cuts through the current with practiced precision, the bronze glow of his current flaring in rhythmic pulses across his armor. His strikes are clean, controlled—too measured for the chaos surrounding him. When he sees me, his light flickers, breaking its pattern.

He fights his way toward me, dodging a burst of static that splits the water in two. His shoulder guard smokes where it caught a near hit, the metal warped and glowing faintly red.

He grabs my wrist, pulling me upright against the flow, eyes wide with disbelief. "You shouldn't be here!"

"I can't just watch them tear each other apart!"

"They're not listening anymore!" he shouts. "Walder's calling for a full breach—the Heartwake's defenses are open! The Flowed will try to seal it!"

"No," I breathe. "If they do that, the pressure will—"

The trench erupts.

A column of energy bursts upward, cutting through the battlefield like lightning made solid. The impact throws us backward. I twist midfall, pushing against the current, and see the aftermath: half the Drains' front line scattered, their bodies spinning through the water like torn banners.

The Lurean soldiers regroup quickly. The air around their weapons glows with captured current, manipulated through gold-lined conduits. They fire again—bursts of compressed energy that explode into spiraling pressure waves. The noise is unbearable, like the sound of the ocean itself breaking apart.

Walder answers with fury.

He spreads his arms, and the sea bends toward him. The coral vines lash out, striking through the ranks of the Flowed. Their golden barriers flare, barely holding. The deeper he draws, the stronger the fissure glows. The Heartwake's pulse begins to sync with his own.

The balance collapses.

“Maren!” Tarek yells, shaking me from my trance. “We have to move before the currents collapse!”

But I can’t move. My gaze is locked on the Heartwake below—the crack in the seafloor, now wide as a canyon. Its glow pulses faster, hotter, as though the battle feeds it. The energy radiating from it stings my skin, filling the water with electric heat.

Every living thing in the trench can feel it—the shift from power to hunger.

“I can stop it,” I whisper.

Tarek’s eyes widen. “Maren—no!”

But I’m already swimming downward. The currents part around me, as though recognizing me, and for one heartbeat, everything slows. The lights, the sound, the chaos—all distant, muffled beneath the rising thrum of the Heartwake.

When I reach the fissure’s edge, the glow is blinding. The molten light rises in long, curling streams that wrap around my arms and tail like tendrils. My veins answer, lighting in rhythm.

I can feel both armies now—their fear, their fury. The Drains’ wild defiance. The Flowed’s desperation to hold control. And at the center of it all, the Heartwake calling my name.

Maren.

The voice is everywhere—in the water, in my chest, in the trembling of the fissure itself.

Let me breathe through you.

I press my hands against the molten edge, pain flaring instantly through my skin. "If I do this," I whisper, "I'll end them all."

Or save them.

The fissure convulses. The water around it twists into spirals of light, swirling faster, brighter. I see Walder in the distance, shouting something, his current flaring in alarm. Tarek is fighting his way toward me, eyes wide, mouth forming my name.

The Heartwake surges.

I reach inward—to the Spark, to the current that has always been both curse and question—and let it rise. The electricity in my veins bursts outward, a living storm that spreads through the water in concentric waves. Every pulse of my heart sends another surge. The light blinds me.

The armies pause mid-strike, caught in the radiance.

Then, silence.

The Spark explodes.

The shockwave ripples through the sea, too fast to see, too powerful to stop. Pressure folds in on itself. Shields shatter. Weapons disintegrate. The coral roots splinter into dust. The fissure beneath me fractures open with a sound like thunder, sending molten light spiraling upward.

The Heartwake screams—a sound felt more than heard—and its outer shell splits, releasing a torrent of energy that tears through the trench.

I'm thrown backward, my vision filled with fragments of light and water and faces. Walder's body spinning through the current. Tarek reaching for me, mouth open in a soundless shout.

The sea collapses inward.

The last thing I feel before everything goes white is the Pulse—the ocean's heart—stopping for a single, impossible beat.

And then nothing.

Only light.

It swallows everything—the sea, the screams, even the sound of my own breath. There's no water anymore, no pressure or gravity, only a flood of brightness so vast it feels alive.

It pours through me, not around me. Every cell burns with it, glowing from the inside out. My body is weightless and weightful all at once, suspended in something that isn't quite water but remembers being it.

Colors shift behind my closed eyes: blue bleeding into gold, then white, then something beyond white—a brilliance that feels sentient. The light hums in waves, steady and deep, pulsing with rhythm. The rhythm becomes a heartbeat. Not mine. Not the ocean's. Something older.

For a moment, I think I hear voices inside it. A thousand whispers layered together, overlapping, rising and falling like a current. Some sound familiar—Zeke's, my mother's, even Tarek's—but they stretch and distort until they become something else. Something unified.

The edges of me dissolve. My hands, my tail, my name—all melt into the radiance. There's no sense of body anymore, only pulse. I drift through it, through the echoes of all the sea's memories—the first spark of life, the first heartbeat beneath the waves, the moment the coral began to sing.

I see flashes: ancient hands weaving current into form; light being born inside darkness; cities of coral rising and collapsing in endless rhythm. The ocean's history folds in on itself, layering over mine until I can't tell where it ends.

The voice—her voice—finds me there.

Maren.

It doesn't echo. It vibrates through the light, through me, smooth and resonant like sound carried through bone.

"Navedia," I whisper, though I don't know if I still have a mouth to speak with.

The sea remembers its shape. You helped it remember.

The light around me brightens, stretching into spirals, each one moving in time with her words. I reach for one, and my hand dissolves into it. For a heartbeat, I see her—eyes of molten fire, hair flowing like liquid gold, her form both human and vast.

"Why me?"

Because you could hold both halves without breaking.

Her voice softens, almost tender. *The sea built itself to survive change. It forgot how. Now it will learn again.*

The light begins to dim, contracting around me. The warmth drains away, leaving only the slow, rhythmic pulse of the Heartwake.

Maren. Her tone fades to a whisper. *Breathe. Return. The current still needs you.*

And just like that, the light begins to fall apart—fracturing into a thousand shimmering pieces that sink around me like dust in water. I reach for them, but they slip through my fingers, vanishing one by one until the glow becomes shadow again.

When I open my eyes, there's no sound. No weight. Only stillness.

The battlefield is gone. The trench is gone.

And before me—through the haze of light—I see her.

Her form shimmers in the water, half human, half light, the edges of her body dissolving into the current itself. Her eyes are the same molten gold as the fissure.

"You broke it," she says, her voice soft but vast. "The shell that held the sea's first breath."

"I didn't mean to," I whisper.

She smiles faintly. "No one ever does."

"What happens now?"

Her gaze drifts upward, toward the surface far above. "Now, the sea learns to breathe again. Whether it survives the inhale depends on you."

The light dims around us. I feel the pull of gravity again, the faint hum of returning current. The war hasn't ended—it's just been rewritten.

As I sink into the fading glow, one truth anchors itself in my chest: I may have saved them both. Or doomed us all.

The silence stretches between us, thick as sediment. Tarek's light flickers faintly in the dim water, painting shifting gold across my skin. I can't stop trembling. Every time the Spark pulses, the world flinches with me—the coral veins in the walls, the sand beneath my tail, even the water itself quivers like it's listening.

Tarek steadies a hand on my shoulder. "Hey. Look at me."

I do, and in the reflection of his eyes, I see how bad it is. The light coming off me isn't just glow—it's alive, writhing like lightning searching for air. My skin is mapped with it, glowing fissures branching down my arms, curling toward my hands.

He swallows hard. "You're burning from the inside."

"It's not pain," I whisper, though my voice is shaking. "It's pressure. Like the sea's pushing through me. Like I can *feel*it."

He doesn't let go. His fingers are warm against the cold surge of current crawling over my skin. "Maren, you have to anchor. Breathe through it, the way you did before."

"I can't." The words break on my tongue. "There's nothing to breathe *with*. The water's dead."

He's quiet for a moment, tail flicking slowly to keep them both suspended. "Then you use mine."

Before I can ask what he means, his hand moves from my shoulder to my chest, over the faint light at the center of me. His current flows through his palm—bronze and steady, a slow hum that feels like heartbeat made visible.

The Spark inside me flares at the contact, startled but listening.

"Let it mirror me," he murmurs, his forehead pressing against mine. "Just follow the rhythm."

I close my eyes. At first it's chaos—too much heat, too much light. But then, under all of that, I feel it: his pulse. Constant. Grounded. It threads through me, wrapping itself around the wildness inside until the two rhythms start to align.

The pain doesn't fade; it changes shape. It becomes movement. The energy stops thrashing and begins to flow, looping through us both in one continuous line. The current finally breathes.

I gasp, and the water moves with me. A ripple spreads outward, subtle but real. The nearest coral flickers, color bleeding faintly back into its surface. Not much—but enough.

Tarek exhales in relief. "There. You're—gods, you're doing it."

I open my eyes, tears slipping free and dissolving instantly into the current. "I don't even know what I'm doing."

He almost smiles. "Then maybe stop trying to."

We drift there, still joined by his touch, surrounded by the faint heartbeat of returning current. But the longer it lasts, the heavier it feels. The Spark isn't calming—it's *waiting*. The Pulse inside me is too big, too vast, stretching beyond anything my body can hold.

I can see it when I look at the world around us: color blooming and fading, like the ocean is exhaling and inhaling unevenly. The coral doesn't know whether to live or die. Neither do I.

Tarek must see the shift in my expression because his hand tightens on mine. "What?"

"It's not over," I whisper. "The Spark isn't settling. It's searching."

"For what?"

I look toward the faint glow of the upper currents—far above, where the old gods once watched and the Flowed still believe they do. "For connection. The sea can't stand still forever. If it can't find the gods, it'll find *me*."

He shakes his head. "You can't carry that alone."

"I already am."

The pain pulses again, sharper this time. My body jerks, and a surge of light bursts from my back, scattering through the still water like shooting stars. The Hollow flares with it—sudden, blinding—then collapses back into dim silence.

Tarek grabs my face, eyes fierce now. "Listen to me. You can't fix this by drowning in it. Whatever your mother started, whatever the Heartwake wants—you're still *you*."

His words hit somewhere deep, grounding and unsteady all at once. I breathe through my teeth, fighting to contain the current building under my ribs.

"The sea's changing," I say. "It's waking up. And it's angry, Tarek. I can *feel* it."

He nods slowly, still holding me. "Then we change with it."

I stare at him, searching his face for fear—but there's none. Just quiet conviction. He's already decided to stand with me, even as the sea decides whether to rebuild or devour itself.

The silence around us deepens. Then, faintly, a current stirs—a soft pull against my skin, hesitant but real. I feel it like a breath at the back of my neck, cautious and alive. The water moves again.

The ocean exhales.

Tarek's hand slips from my chest, but his gaze doesn't. "Whatever happens next," he says softly, "we do it together."

I nod, the Spark still pulsing beneath my skin, wild and restless.

Together.

But even as I say it, I know the truth burning underneath the calm: this isn't the end of the storm. It's the moment before it remembers how to rage.

CHAPTER FIFTEEN

The Light

I dream of air again.

It comes to me in flashes—blue sky so bright it hurts, the sound of waves breaking against sand, light that doesn't refract but burns clean and sharp. I can *feel* it on my face, that strange, dry warmth I've never truly known but that lives somewhere in my blood.

The world above is impossibly still. I'm standing where sea meets sky, but the tide doesn't touch my feet. The horizon stretches endlessly, a mirror of gold and silver. When I look down, I have legs—long and unsteady, unfamiliar in their grace.

They shimmer faintly where the scales used to be, as though the sea hasn't decided whether to let me go. I take a step, and the sand gives beneath me, warm and alive.

A voice ripples through the still air—low, distant, and not quite sound. *You were never meant to choose one world over the other*.

I turn, but no one's there. Only the light shifting across the waves.

"Mother?" I whisper, and the horizon answers with silence.

Then the sky fractures. The color drains. The sea folds inward, collapsing into the shape of an eye—vast and glowing, the color of molten coral.

The world inhales—then shatters. The sea folds inward, its weight collapsing through me as if every drop remembers gravity. Light surges upward in a single, blinding column. My body lifts, carried by the pull, every bone and thought untethered.

There is no current now, no direction, no breath. Just motion—endless and without shape.

I tumble through it, limbs suspended, the water around me liquefying into color. The blue becomes white, the white becomes gold, and then there's nothing but the taste of salt and the echo of a heartbeat that doesn't belong to me.

Images flash through the brightness—faces I know, places I love—Zeke reaching toward me from a corridor of broken coral, my father's hands clenching the arms of his throne, my mother's eyes illuminated from within. The Hollow disintegrates around them, turning into ribbons of light that unravel and reform in a rhythm I can almost understand.

The sea isn't gone. It's *turning inside out*.

Currents thread through the void like veins of fire, pulling fragments of the world together again. I try to call out, but my voice is only vibration. The sound becomes a ripple of light, scattering into the vastness.

Somewhere beyond it, something answers.

A voice—not words, but thought—slides through me, familiar and too close. *Maren. You are not falling. You are being remembered.*

I reach for the sound, for her, but the light thickens around my hand. The pressure climbs, hot and electric, until I can't tell whether I'm burning or breathing.

I try to fight it. I try to *breathe*, but the light fills my lungs. It moves through me the way water does—everywhere, infinite, alive.

The sea's pulse beats once, hard enough to shake the stars from their places.

Then the world collapses again—quiet this time, soft as an exhale. The light condenses, drawing inward until it's all pressed behind my eyelids, waiting.

And when I open them, I wake choking on light.

For one heartbeat, I don't know where I am. The walls around me are trembling with faint gold, the veins of the Hollow flickering back to life. The water stings, hot against my skin.

Tarek is gone.

When I push myself upright, the current resists—thick, heavy, full of sediment. The faint thrum of the Heartwake beats through the stone like a pulse deep underfoot.

A noise cuts through the silence—an echoing flare, high and clear, carried through the dead current. It takes me a moment to understand it's not sound but signal. A beacon.

Someone is *coming*.

I swim to the nearest glass corridor and peer through the fractured wall. And there—rising from the trench's lowest ridge—comes a column of soft, pink-gold light.

Not Walder. Not Navedia.

My mother.

Her current blazes weak but steady, spiraling upward from the Trench's base like a tether of breath. She's moving toward the Heartwake, her body outlined by the dim glow of molten coral.

I race through the Hollow, following the light. Each corridor feels longer than the last, as if the sea itself is stretching to hold me back. The ache in my chest grows with every stroke.

When I finally reach the fissure's edge, she's already there.

Selara hovers before the Heartwake, her body illuminated from within. The coral embedded in her skin glows faintly through her chest and throat, casting her features in fragile light. Her lungs—once strong, alive—now flicker unevenly, petals of coral curling and cracking with each breath.

"Mother," I breathe.

She turns, and I see her smile. Not the careful one she wore at court, not the pained one from the last memory I have of her. A real smile.

"Maren," she says, her voice softer than the current. "You heard him, didn't you? Your father's plea."

I nod, my throat tight. "He said you escaped. I thought—"

"That I ran?" she finishes for me, with a faint laugh that turns into a cough. The cracks along her collarbone deepen, light leaking from within. "I didn't escape, love. I came home."

She looks past me, to the Heartwake's fractured glow. "It's unraveling. The sea's pulse is collapsing under the weight of two wills—Navedia's and yours. It can't hold both."

"I can fix it," I say quickly. "You don't have to—"

Her gaze cuts through me. "Yes, you can. But not alone."

She swims closer, every movement labored, her breath rattling. The coral in her lungs flares with every word. "The binding that kept me alive is breaking. I can feel the coral pulling free. It wants to return to the Heartwake—to where it began."

"No." The word fractures in the water. "You can't. You'll die."

Her hand finds my cheek, trembling but warm. "I was never meant to live this long. The coral doesn't belong inside a human body. It was meant to breathe with the sea, not against it."

She takes a slow, shallow breath. "When it fuses back into the Heartwake, it will buy you time. Enough for you to reclaim what Navedia stole."

"Mother, please—"

"Maren." Her voice sharpens, soft but unyielding. "I spent my life trying to save you from what you are. Now I understand—it's not something to fear. The Spark was never meant to be mine. It's yours. And the sea will only listen if you make it remember."

Her glow brightens, filling the trench with rose-colored light. Cracks spread across her arms and throat, thin lines of gold that shimmer like veins of sunlight in water. The sight tears through me.

"Don't do this," I beg. "Please."

She leans forward, pressing her forehead against mine. "You once told me you felt trapped beneath the sea. That you dreamed of seeing the surface. Remember what I said?"

I nod, barely.

"That the ocean has a surface, yes–but even light must travel through darkness to reach it."

Her smile deepens, her eyes shining. "Now let me be that light."

She pulls away before I can stop her. Her arms rise, and the coral embedded in her skin begins to unfurl, peeling free like threads of living flame. They drift from her body in ribbons, drawn toward the fissure's core. The Heartwake responds instantly–its dim glow surging to life, tendrils of molten color coiling upward to meet her offering.

"Mother!" I scream, swimming forward.

The pressure slams into me, hurling me backward. The light is blinding now, burning gold and rose and blue all at once. Through it, I see her–floating in the center of the fissure, arms spread, body dissolving into radiant coral light.

The coral essence fuses into the Heartwake, knitting through the fractures Navedia's influence left behind. The fissure seals in slow, radiant motion, its cracks glowing brighter than I've ever seen.

The sea trembles. The water breathes again.

I fall to my knees, the current rippling outward. My vision blurs with salt and grief. Through the glow, I can still see her shape—just barely—suspended in the molten light like part of it.

And then she is gone.

No body. No blood. Only light.

The glow settles deep within the Heartwake, gentle and steady, beating like a heart.

Tarek finds me moments later, his voice shaking when he whispers, “What happened?”

“She gave herself back,” I say, my words breaking on the edges of the current.

He kneels beside me, staring at the radiant fissure. “Then the sea...”

“...is alive,” I finish.

The water hums again, a slow, familiar rhythm. Coral begins to glow faintly along the trench walls, their color returning in slow waves. The current drifts through the Hollow like breath after near-drowning.

I look down, toward the glowing depths where my mother’s light lingers. It flickers softly at first, like the last breath before sleep, then steadies—an unwavering pulse in the dark. The water around it glows warmer, carrying color back into the stone, coaxing life into the coral veins that had gone gray.

Selara isn’t gone. She’s become the sea’s pulse—its memory, its mercy. I can feel her still, a rhythm under my ribs that isn’t mine alone. Every wave that brushes my skin carries a trace of her voice, every ripple hums with the shape of her love. The ache in my chest doesn’t fade, but it changes—less wound, more tether.

The Queen of Lurea now reigns in silence and light, her body dissolved into the current, her spirit threaded through every heartbeat of the ocean she saved. And though grief tightens around me, I know she isn't lost.

She is the sea now.

And as the Heartwake glows steady once more, I realize—I will never swim without her again.

CHAPTER SIXTEEN
The Crown

The current carries me upward through the trench, past the glow of the Heartwake, past the molten walls still trembling with my mother's light. The water is warm around me, heavy with the residue of her sacrifice. The farther I rise, the colder it becomes—thin and sharp, filled with echoes of what once was divine order.

The sea feels different now.

I swim upward through the dim bands of depth, the trench narrowing behind me. The silence that once pressed against my ribs has lifted, replaced by a hum that's neither sound nor current—something deeper, a vibration that moves through the marrow of the water itself. The Heartwake's glow still lingers far below, a wound of light pulsing steadily in the dark. I can feel its rhythm in my chest, each beat carrying a fragment of my mother's last breath.

The ascent is long. The water grows colder, thinner. My movements leave small trails of bioluminescence that cling to my skin before fading, as though the sea wants to mark my passing. Schools of silver fish drift near, unbothered by my presence, following alongside me for a few heartbeats before scattering into the haze.

Above, faint shafts of light pierce through the blue. The Hollow's reach thins, and the open expanse of the upper ocean unfurls before me—a place that feels both foreign and familiar, as if the sea is rearranging its memory to make room for something new.

I pass through the ruins of the old currentways, their glass veins cracked but glowing faintly, fed by the pulse rising from below. Coral gardens bend toward the trench, their tendrils catching the shimmer of the revived current. Even the broken towers breathe again—slowly, cautiously—like the city itself is deciding whether to trust the light.

The journey feels endless. Every shadow looks like memory, every echo like the ghost of a name I once knew. The deeper I swim into the midwaters, the more I sense the shift. The ocean is restless, alive in a way it's never been before. The gods' silence is absolute now, but it isn't empty. It's full of watching.

When I pass the outer guards of Lurea, they don't move. Their armor glints faintly, weapons drawn but unused, eyes fixed on the glow spreading from the depths below. They don't even call my name. They just watch me drift by, as though I'm something half-familiar and half divine.

The city unfolds ahead—towers of coral and glass, all painted with the soft gold of returning light. But it's different now. The currents around it have lost their order. The delicate spirals that once guided the flow are breaking apart, reforming into new paths. The sea's design is rewriting itself, and no one knows what it will become.

By the time I breach the upper ridge, the Hollow's light has spread across the trench like sunrise. Word of the Queen's rebirth—though none dare call it that yet—has already reached the city. I can feel it in the currents: confusion, awe, fear. The world is holding its breath.

The Council waits.

They've gathered in the Amphicourt beneath the Crown Wave, the barrier that crowns Lurea's capital—a dome of living current woven by the priests centuries ago, said to carry the sea gods' will. It hums faintly above the marble dais, a shimmer of gold and blue that ripples whenever someone speaks the old prayers.

I can taste its charge from here.

Tarek swims at my side but keeps his distance now, knowing this moment isn't meant to be shared. "They'll call it treason," he murmurs.

"They already have," I answer.

When I step into the chamber, the crowd parts. Not for reverence—out of instinct. My glow still hasn't dimmed since the Heartwake. Every motion leaves a faint trail of light, as though the sea itself is reluctant to let me pass unnoticed.

At the center of the dais stands my father, King Thalen of Lurea—robes torn, crown tilted, the weight of a dying faith in his eyes. The coral veins running along the walls flicker weakly, their color fading in and out like a failing heartbeat. Around him hover the Depth Council, a circle of nobles and priests clutching relics of the old gods, their faces drawn with fear masquerading as piety.

"Maren."

His voice carries through the water, deeper than I remember, softened by something almost human.

I bow my head, but not in deference. "Father."

"You've returned." His gaze flicks briefly to Tarek, then to the glow still emanating from my chest. "And you've brought the storm with you."

I let the silence stretch. "The Heartwake lives again. The sea breathes because of Mother."

His jaw tightens. "Your mother defied the gods. Her sacrifice was not a blessing—it was rebellion."

"Rebellion?" My voice cracks with disbelief. "She gave herself to the ocean so it could live. The gods abandoned us, Father. She didn't."

A priest behind him snarls, clutching his relic tighter. "Blasphemy! The stilling was punishment for the Sparkblood's corruption—"

"Enough." Thalen raises a hand, silencing them. "Maren. You will end this. The Drains still fight in your name. The Heartwake's power spreads unchecked. You will surrender your Spark to the priests, and we will seal it within the Vault."

"You can't seal the sea," I say quietly.

He looks at me then—not as a king, but as a father who no longer recognizes the child before him. "You are not the sea."

"Then what am I?"

His mouth opens, but no answer comes. The silence between us widens until it feels like the whole ocean could drown in it.

Finally, he says, "You are my daughter. That is why I am asking instead of commanding."

"You're asking me to die," I whisper.

He doesn't deny it.

Behind him, the Crown Wave hums louder. The priests raise their tridents in unison, murmuring the ancient words that bind the throne's divine barrier. The dome above the dais brightens, filling the water with gold and heat. Its power has always felt distant, celestial—but now, it burns close and small, the way dying things do when they try to seem alive.

I stare past the shimmer of the barrier to my father's face, searching for something—grief, regret, anything. But his expression is carved in stone. He stands tall, the posture of a king who refuses to look down into the wreckage he's caused.

"She's gone," I whisper. "You didn't even try to find her."

Thalen's eyes flicker, the smallest tremor beneath the practiced calm. "Your mother made her choice."

"Her choice?" My voice rises, the water vibrating with it. "To sacrifice herself for the sea? Or to live in your shadow while you called her salvation blasphemy?"

He straightens, the faintest flare of anger in his current. "You speak of things you do not understand. Selara was... devoted. But she forgot her place."

"Her *place*?" The word burns my throat. "Do you mean her cell, or the laboratory you banished her to when her lungs began to fail?"

A muscle tightens along his jaw. "Enough."

I swim forward, the water around me trembling. "You call her rebellion, but she was dying, Father. Dying, and still trying to save you, to save *all of this.*" I gesture to the grand chamber, to the coral walls dulled by fear, to the flickering veins of the Crown Wave that now pulse erratically. "She gave herself to keep the sea alive, and you stand here pretending she was a threat to your gods. Were you ever proud of her? Did you ever love her, or just the control she gave you?"

He recoils as if struck. The mask slips—pain flashing across his face before pride snaps it shut again. "How dare you?" he says softly, voice trembling like a cracked blade. "Everything I have done has been for this kingdom, for this family. You think love means abandoning faith? You think I could watch her tear apart the covenant and call it devotion?"

"She wasn't tearing it apart," I hiss. "She was *rebuilding it!* The gods turned away, Father. Mother didn't."

His eyes flash, and for a moment, I see not a king but a man drowning in the world he built. "The gods do not need us to understand them. They demand obedience, not interpretation. That is the order she defied—and now you follow her into ruin."

I stop, breath ragged, the ache in my chest spreading into my hands. "She died believing you still might listen."

The words hang between us, sharp and final. His lips part, but no sound comes. For all his fury, all his faith, he has nothing to say to that.

The silence hurts worse than any strike.

Behind him, the Crown Wave thrums louder, sensing the rising tension. The priests tighten their formation, tridents raised, their chants quickening to drown out the argument. Gold threads shimmer through the dome's surface, pulsing like veins under too-thin skin. The light presses against my eyes, hot and oppressive, filling the chamber with the scent of charged salt.

The Council murmurs uneasily, their voices overlapping in broken prayers. I can feel their fear—of me, of the sea, of what's coming.

I swim closer to it. The water shudders in my wake, the light of the barrier bending toward me as if the sea itself is holding its breath. My father's hand twitches, half reaching for me, torn between command and instinct, between king and father.

"Maren," he warns, voice low. "Don't."

I look up at the Crown Wave, its surface trembling like breath caught between sob and scream. "You told me this barrier was the gods' will," I say softly. "That it protected us from the chaos below."

"It *does,*" Thalen says.

"Then tell me why it trembles when I breathe."

The priests' chanting grows louder. The light of the barrier pulses faster, reacting to the Spark thrumming under my skin. I lift my hand. The water thickens. The current bends. The glow from my chest flares bright enough to paint every face in the chamber blue.

"Maren—stop!" my father shouts.

I press my palm to the barrier.

The Crown Wave flares in protest, a blinding eruption of gold that surges through the chamber. The priests recoil as lightning arcs between their tridents, searing the water. The sound is like coral splitting—clean, irreversible.

For one suspended moment, the barrier holds.

Then it *tears*.

A fissure rips through its center, light spilling outward in wild threads. The sound rolls through the city, through the palace, through the sea itself. The golden shell splinters, dissolving into ribbons that spiral downward and fade.

The divine current—the one that kept the throne's covenant alive for generations—is gone.

The water stills.

I lower my hand, the glow receding. "The sea doesn't recognize the Covenant anymore," I say softly. "It answers to no throne."

The chamber erupts in shouts. The priests scatter, their relics useless. Members of the Council flee through the corridors, calling for guards who won't come.

Thalen stands unmoving, staring at the empty space where the barrier used to be. His crown tilts, one of its coral prongs cracked.

Zeke bursts through the doors then, armor half-buckled, eyes wide. "Father—Maren—what did you—?"

He freezes when he sees the shattered Crown Wave. His gaze moves from me to Thalen, then back again. "Where's Mother?"

The question lands like a wound. I open my mouth, but no words come.

Thalen answers instead, voice breaking. "She's gone. She gave herself to the sea's madness."

Zeke's jaw tightens. "No. Not madness." His voice steadies, low but fierce. "She *saved* it."

"Zeke—"

He turns toward me, eyes full of something I've never seen in him before—clarity. "She did, didn't she?"

I nod. "She became the Pulse."

He looks back at our father, shoulders squaring. "Then everything you've told us—everything about the gods, about order, about the Covenant—it's a lie."

Thalen's expression hardens, but I can see the cracks spreading there too.

Zeke swims to my side. "You're right, Maren. The sea doesn't belong to them anymore."

The silence that follows is deep, ringing, heavy with what's been broken. The great throne behind my father—carved from coral and stone older than the city itself—splinters down the center with a sound like a held breath finally released.

The fissure glows faintly blue.

Thalen stumbles back, eyes wide, crown slipping from his brow. The light spreads along the cracks, threading through the dais and the walls until the entire chamber hums with low, living current.

The Covenant is undone. The throne fractures—literally and symbolically. Since the sea began, the current belongs to no one but itself.

CHAPTER SEVENTEEN

The Storm

The light shatters before the sound reaches us.

One heartbeat, the Crown Wave flickers—its veins pulsing a feverish gold. The next, every current in the chamber reverses. The water snaps inward, collapsing toward the Heartwake miles below, dragging with it the breath of the sea.

Then the world explodes.

The wave hits Lurea like a living thing. The palace walls convulse, sending spirals of coral and dust through the current. The priests' chants die mid-phrase as the water thickens, growing heavy and electric. Every light in the chamber flickers out.

And then she comes.

Not in form, not in flesh—*in everything*.

The sea itself ignites, turning the water into a storm of molten blue and gold. Light bursts from the cracks in the dais, racing along the walls in serpentine motion, converging at the heart of the chamber. The current roars, alive and wordless, pressing against my chest until it feels like my ribs might splinter.

I know that presence. I've felt it in my bones since the first surge beneath the Hollow. Her voice isn't sound—it's force. Every drop of water vibrates with her will. The chamber trembles, the world bending around her awakening.

Daughter of Spark and Flesh, the voice resounds, resonant and vast. *You opened the gate. You broke the shell that bound me. The sea remembers its mother.*

Tarek collapses to one knee, clutching his head. The Council cries out, their relics sparking uselessly against the onslaught of current. My father staggers backward, eyes wide, crown slipping.

"Gods," he whispers.

"No," I breathe. "Just one."

The Heartwake's light spears through the floor—blue and endless—and from it rises a figure made of current and fire, flickering, shifting, too bright to hold shape. She is a storm given sentience, an ocean given face.

Maren, she says, and this time, it sounds like love.

Her voice floods my body, filling the spaces between my thoughts. I see her memories as my own—seas being born, coral breathing for the first time, the old gods kneeling before her pulse. I see the wars that broke her, the covenants that caged her light, and finally, her waiting—centuries of silence, until my mother's coral lungs carried a piece of her essence back into the world.

"You called me your daughter," I say. My voice trembles with the current. "But I was born of blood."

Blood is salt, and salt is sea. You are both, she answers. *You can end this. Merge with me. Become what the sea was meant to be before mortals divided it. One will, one voice, one endless tide.*

The offer wraps around me like warmth. The water calms. The storm eases. I feel no separation—no difference between breath and current, between me and the deep.

It feels like peace.

The Spark within me flares, answering hers. The light in the chamber swells until the edges of everything blur. I can feel the pull—vast and sweet and inevitable. If I let go, the pain would vanish. The conflict. The hunger. There would only be oneness, eternal and unbroken.

"Maren!"

Tarek's voice cuts through the water, distant and desperate. I can barely see him through the glow. His silhouette reaches toward me, small against the vastness. Behind him, Zeke is shouting something, fighting to hold his footing as the current drags him toward the dais.

Navedia's light curls around me like a tide, her voice soft and endless. *Let them go. Let the sea begin again. You will never be alone.*

And for a heartbeat, I believe her.

I see it—the vision of a perfect ocean: no kings, no gods, no walls between water and sky. A sea where everything moves as one pulse. Harmony.

But then—my mother's voice, faint but clear, drifts through the current.
Harmony isn't sameness, Maren. It's survival.

The memory cuts through the trance like a blade. Her face flickers behind my eyes—Selara, smiling through the light of the Heartwake, her body dissolving into the coral veins. She gave herself not to control the sea, but to give it choice.

I look back at Navedia's storm. Her light ripples with expectation.

"You said the sea remembers its mother," I whisper. "But mothers don't keep their children—they let them grow."

The warmth shifts. Navedia's voice turns sharper, quieter. *Without me, it will drown again.*

"Maybe it has to," I say.

I reach inward. The Spark within me trembles, alive and wild. I turn it—not outward, but inward—folding the current back into my body. The pressure builds instantly, light and pain colliding in my chest. The water shrieks, energy twisting in on itself.

Navedia screams—a sound that makes the sea convulse. Her form lashes out, blinding arcs of light tearing through the chamber. The floor cracks beneath me. The Heartwake howls.

But I hold the current close. My pulse and hers overlap until I can't tell them apart, then *split* them, forcing the energy apart, dividing the inheritance she's trying to claim. The Spark burns through me, searing my veins with light.

I don't destroy her. I unmake her shape.

The storm convulses, collapsing inward like a dying wave. The golden fire dissolves, unraveling into the sea it once ruled. The light thins. The voice fades.

When it's done, only silence remains—heavy and clean.

I fall to my knees, every muscle trembling, my body still glowing faintly from within. The water around me feels lighter, freer, like a held breath finally released.

The Heartwake stabilizes, its glow dimming into a calm, steady pulse. The chamber, once radiant and violent, now flickers with soft blue light.

Tarek rushes to my side, catching me before I collapse. "Maren," he breathes, "what did you—?"

I shake my head weakly. "I ended it. The sea's inheritance. The gods. The Covenant. All of it."

Zeke hovers nearby, staring at the fading light. "So it's over?"

I manage a faint, trembling smile. "No," I whisper. "It's beginning."

Around us, the broken throne lies in silence, half-buried in the sand. The coral veins that once marked divine rule now pulse faintly—not gold, but blue.

The sea no longer answers to gods. It breathes on its own, and as I feel the Spark settle within me, quieter but alive, I finally understand what my mother meant.

Harmony is coexistence.

The silence afterward feels enormous. The sea is utterly still. The current curls around me like breath, soft and slow, and I realize how long it's been since I've heard it without fear in its voice.

Tarek's hand stays on my shoulder. His pulse is faint, but steady, grounding me when the last echoes of the Heartwake fade from my veins. I'm trembling—part exhaustion, part awe. The light beneath my skin has dimmed, but it hasn't gone. It lingers, quiet, like an ember that knows it doesn't have to burn to exist.

"The storm's gone," Tarek says. "So… what now?"

I take a breath, or something like it, feeling the water move in time with me. The Heartwake's glow below has changed—no longer pulsing with heat or hunger, but with rhythm. My mother's rhythm.

"I don't know," I admit. "Maybe now the sea finally decides for itself."

He studies me, a faint smile tugging at his mouth. "You sound like her."

The words hit harder than he means them to, but I let the ache come. It's not grief anymore—not exactly. It's something warmer, deeper, like the sea finally settling into its own heartbeat.

Around us, the chamber begins to heal. The shattered coral along the dais is knitting itself together, soft veins of blue crawling across the stone where gold once burned. The priests have fled; the Council's relics lie scattered on the floor, their lights extinguished. Only my father and brother remain.

Thalen stands near the broken throne, his crown gone, the faint glow of the old gods' current long faded from his robes. He's just a man now, stripped of myth. His eyes find mine, and I see the weight in them—the kind that can't be commanded away.

"Maren," he says quietly. There's no power in it anymore, just fatigue.

I drift closer, but not too close. "You can't rebuild what's gone," I tell him.

He nods slowly, gaze falling to the shattered coral beneath his feet. "Then maybe I shouldn't try."

Something in me softens. For so long, I thought I wanted him to bow, to *see* what he'd done. But now, standing before what's left of his rule, I realize he already has.

Zeke swims to my side. He looks different now—his armor cracked, his glow dim but steady. The anger that once burned behind his eyes has cooled into resolve. "You were right," he says simply. "Mother wasn't destroying the sea. She was saving it. I see that now."

I nod. "She believed in its capacity to change."

"So do I."

He turns toward the fractured dais, pressing his hand against the wall where the Crown Wave used to hum. For a heartbeat, nothing happens. Then faint light blooms beneath his palm—not gold, but silver, quiet and soft.

The sea still answers us—but differently now.

Tarek glances upward, toward the open currentways where faint light seeps through the cracks. "They'll be afraid," he says. "The Drains, the Flowed, all of them. Without the gods, without a throne..."

"They'll have to learn to listen to each other," I say. "The sea won't choose sides anymore."

"And you?" he asks softly.

I look down at my hands, where the last traces of light fade into skin. "I'll listen too."

The current brushes against my cheek—gentle, familiar. Somewhere far below, the Heartwake glows again, steady as a heartbeat. I imagine my mother's voice carried through it, not as command or prophecy, but as lullaby.

I swim upward, toward the broken crown that hangs suspended in the still water, its coral glinting faintly in the new light. It's strange how small it looks now—fragile, almost human. I touch it once, not to claim it, but to release it.

It drifts away, carried by the current.

When I turn back, Tarek and Zeke are watching me. Neither speaks. They don't have to.

We drift together in the center of what used to be the throne room, the water around us finally calm. The sea hums faintly—not the chant of priests, not the murmur of gods, but the pulse of life finding new rhythm. I don't feel like I'm at war with it.

The ocean doesn't belong to thrones, or covenants, or even gods anymore. It belongs to itself; and so do I.

CHAPTER EIGHTEEN
The Currents

For a long while, the sea is quiet—too quiet, the kind that comes before something remembers how to move.

I float at the center of what remains of the throne chamber, the water thick with the residue of light. The cracks in the coral glow faintly, no longer gold but blue-white, the same shade that lives beneath my skin. The Heartwake's pulse hums faintly below, weak but alive. The sea is breathing again, but its rhythm falters—unsteady, uncertain, like a newborn learning its lungs.

Tarek hovers behind me, his presence steady but distant. Zeke lingers near the edge of the dais, his hand pressed against the broken coral, as if he can still hear our mother through it. Neither speaks. They know this is something words can't reach.

The Spark stirs beneath my ribs, restless. It has grown since the battle—expanded beyond my body, beyond even thought. It's not just energy anymore; it's memory, will, connection. I feel it threading through the water, brushing against the lives scattered across the sea. The Drains, the Flowed, the wandering nomads between them—every current, every creature, all of them waiting for something they can't name.

I close my eyes and let go.

The Spark answers instantly, rushing outward like a held breath finally released. My body trembles as the current tears through me, gathering power from the Heartwake's depths and hurling it upward. The sea ignites in light.

The glow races through the trench first—narrow veins of molten blue snaking along the seafloor, threading through the coral pillars like veins beneath translucent skin. The stone itself seems to awaken, fracturing in patterns of light that travel outward, branching into thousands of radiant paths.

From the Hollow below, I hear the deep groan of living coral shifting, expanding as if stretching after a long sleep. The ground ripples under me, breathing. Chunks of shell and crystal rise from the sand, weightless now, spinning slowly in the current.

The first burst of energy hits the water column and splits it apart—beams of gold and silver twisting upward through leagues of ocean. The dark turns clear. Every droplet burns with color, refracting light the way air bends heat. For a moment, I can see the whole sea—every ridge, every crevice, every living thing—as though the water itself has turned to glass.

Then comes the movement.

Currents that had been dead for centuries awaken, stirring in spiral patterns that dance through the ruins of Lurea. They catch on the towers and broken bridges, curling around them like ribbons of flame. The walls of the city flare with phosphorescent light, the old carvings of gods and queens glowing from within. The streets flood with motion again—schools of fish darting through arches, their scales throwing off sparks like molten stars.

The deeper I reach, the wilder it becomes. The surge of light floods through the trench, illuminating creatures that haven't been seen in generations. Massive shapes rise from the abyssal dark—leviathans coiling in slow circles, their eyes burning like lanterns. Columns of glowing plankton swirl around them, caught in their wake, painting spiral galaxies beneath the waves.

Above, the water glows brighter than the surface sky. The beams shoot through layers of current, weaving together into a single, seamless pattern—a lattice of pure energy. I can feel the electricity threading through it, lightning and tide mingling until they become one breath.

Through it all, the sound—deep, resonant, endless. The sea's heartbeat, reborn.

It pulses outward in rings, each one brighter, stronger than the last. The rings expand across the ocean floor, colliding and overlapping in waves of shimmering light. Every pulse changes something: dead coral blooms, gray shells glisten with color, the faint silhouettes of lost wrecks dissolve into drifting gardens of phosphorescent anemone.

Even the light itself begins to evolve—no longer only blue, but streaked with pinks and greens and soft auroras of violet, as if the sea has learned to speak in every color it was once denied. The water vibrates around me, alive with motion and scent—the mineral tang of energy, the sweetness of regrown algae, the heat of rebirth.

At first, it's chaos—flashes of white-blue lightning splitting through the dark, threads of gold spiraling from my hands. The water convulses, and for a moment, I fear I've broken it again. But then the pressure stabilizes, folding into rhythm. The Pulse—the true Pulse—rises.

It's different now. Before, the current always flowed one way, feeding the throne, feeding the gods. Now it turns, bending back on itself, circular and infinite. It surges outward from the Heartwake, rippling through the entire ocean, then returns—energy feeding energy, life feeding life. A living loop.

A current that flows both ways.

I can *feel* it move. It brushes across my skin like warmth and static, sweeping outward in radiant waves. In Lurea, the broken spires spark to life, their coral veins glowing brighter than they ever have. In the Hollow below, the Drains lift their heads, eyes wide as the trenches bloom with color.

The Flowed feel it too. Their shields drop. Their weapons dim. The sea doesn't recognize sides anymore. Every pulse carries the same charge—every creature touched by it, changed by it.

Above the trench, massive shapes begin to rise. Rays the size of ships. Serpents of light winding through the water. Schools of fish glowing in tandem, their bodies flickering in rhythm with the new current. Even the coral itself moves, unfurling tendrils like flowers opening after endless dark.

The ocean is alive again—not restored, but remade.

My body burns with it, the Spark running unchecked through every vein. The energy is too much for one form to contain, but I don't fight it. The current threads through my skin, my hair, my lungs, merging flesh with sea. I can feel it shifting me—bone dissolving into light, scales threading through my blood, the water itself carrying my breath.

Half-human. Half-sea.

The bridge my mother dreamed of—and Navedia tried to claim.

The power hums softly now, pulsing in harmony with the Heartwake. It doesn't consume. It connects.

The vibration spreads outward, gentle at first, then stronger—waves folding through the water like breath. Every surface answers: coral veins lighting, sand shimmering, the faintest creatures pulsing in quiet response. It's not a storm anymore; it's song.

I can feel it everywhere. The sea no longer resists me—it moves *with* me, the way lungs move with breath. Every heartbeat echoes in the current, each one answered by a thousand others. Even the dark places—the deep ridges that once held only silence—glow faintly now, lit from within. The ocean's body is whole again, every fracture mended by rhythm instead of rule.

And in that rhythm, I sense her—my mother's essence threaded through the Heartwake, her light pulsing faintly beneath mine, keeping the flow steady. Her presence no longer aches; it steadies. She hums through the currents like a lullaby learned by the entire sea.

The power ripples once more, expanding beyond my reach, climbing through the endless layers of water. I feel it crest along the ridges of the trenches, race over reefs and gardens, stretch toward the surface where light bends and breaks. The energy warms as it goes, turning the deep into a living prism.

The sea changes shape around me. The old architecture of the palace—its marble spires, its jeweled gates—melts into the water, dissolved by the very current that once sustained it. What's left is purer: light, current, and sound. The ocean has shed its skin.

When I open my eyes, the chamber has vanished. I'm standing in open water, though I no longer need to move to stay afloat. The sea itself holds me aloft. All around me, the light flows upward in long, spiraling beams, each one connected to the next, weaving a tapestry of movement. Beneath me, the Heartwake's glow stretches outward like a second sky inverted.

My reflection shimmers in the water below—skin faintly luminous, eyes bright with the color of storms. My tail has faded into transparency, a living current of light that flickers and reforms with every pulse. I watch as it curls through the water, no longer muscle or fin but energy, shaped by the rhythm of the sea itself.

Above me, the light of the surface trembles, not as barrier but invitation. I don't feel torn between worlds. I *am* both—air and water, pulse and Spark, human and sea.

Tarek drifts forward, awe written across his face. "Maren..."

I smile faintly, though the expression feels foreign, like it belongs to someone larger than I am. "It's done."

"What are you now?" Zeke asks, his voice quiet but steady.

“I don’t know,” I say. “Maybe what the sea needed to become.”

The water glows brighter around us, warm and soft. I can feel the Pulse moving through it, through me, carrying light to every corner of the ocean. I feel the Drains kneeling in reverence, the Flowed looking skyward in wonder, the smallest of fish darting through the illuminated coral. All of it—breathing, living, *being*.

This is what Mother meant. Harmony isn’t sameness. It’s survival.

The current surges once more, flowing outward toward the distant edges of the world. I raise my hand, and the sea answers—not as servant, not as worshipper, but as equal.

The ocean doesn’t belong to gods or crowns anymore. It belongs to itself; and as the light folds around me, threading through every wave and ripple, I understand—

I am not a queen. I am not a god.

I am the bridge. The sea flows through me, and I through it, our heartbeats now the same.

The current stills around me, but it’s not the silence of emptiness—it’s anticipation, as though the ocean itself is holding something just beyond my reach. A ripple brushes against my arm, faint and deliberate, carrying with it a hum that isn’t entirely mine.

I turn.

From the shadows beneath the broken dais, light moves. At first, I think it’s only a reflection of the Heartwake—a trick of the water—but then it shifts again, slow and purposeful. The shape that emerges is like nothing I’ve seen before.

Its body gleams with threads of copper and blue, long fins curling behind it like banners in slow motion. Its eyes are enormous and alive with pale, shifting light—neither predator nor prey, but something older, patient. The glow along its sides pulses faintly, the same hue as my Spark.

It stops a few feet from me, hovering just outside my reach. The current between us vibrates softly, almost shy. "What are you?" I whisper, though the question feels small in the water.

The creature blinks once, and I *feel* the answer more than hear it. A resonance—warm, low, familiar. It's like the sea speaking in color instead of words.

When I lift my hand, the water between us hums, and the creature drifts closer, brushing its head against my palm. Its skin is soft as kelp, smooth as glass. The touch sends a jolt through me—not pain, but recognition.

The Spark inside me flares in response.

Light bursts along its body, rippling outward in spirals of gold and blue that trace symbols across its scales—symbols I've only ever seen etched into the walls of the old sanctuaries, long before they fell to ruin. The creature shivers once, as though remembering, and then goes still again, its glow matching mine beat for beat.

A connection forms instantly, effortless and whole. I can feel its heartbeat echoing through my hand, steady and certain, tethering to mine.

A voice breaks the silence behind me.

"It remembers you," my father says softly.

I turn to see Thalen hovering at the edge of the fractured chamber, crown gone, robes drifting loosely in the current. He looks older now—fragile, hollowed—but there's something in his eyes I've never seen before. Not command. Not pride. Something gentler.

"What do you mean?" I ask, still watching the creature.

He swims closer, careful and slow. "It was found decades ago in the deep sanctum, near the first fissures of the Heartwake. We didn't understand what it was then—only that its light reacted to the Spark. The priests called it dangerous, blasphemous. They said it was a remnant of Navedia's first creation."

His voice falters. "I didn't know what else to do. I ordered it locked away."

I glance down at the creature, which seems impossibly peaceful now, curling its fins lazily in the water, the tips flickering with pale light. The thought of it caged makes my chest tighten.

"You imprisoned it for existing," I say quietly.

Thalen bows his head. "For being beyond my understanding."

There's no defense in his tone this time. Only exhaustion.

"I thought I was protecting the kingdom," he continues. "But I was only protecting my fear. When the barrier fell, the vaults broke open. It was found near the lower cells, waiting. The guards said it refused to leave. Until now."

He gestures toward the creature, and the faintest smile ghosts across his face. "Consider it a gift, Maren.

Not from a king, but from a father who has nothing else left to give."

The creature turns as if it understands. Its light brightens, spilling warmth through the chamber until the coral itself glows in reflection. It swims a slow circle around me, leaving trails of luminous bubbles in its wake.

When it stops again, it lowers its head until its eyes meet mine.

The current between us hums like song. I can *feel* what it is now—not a weapon, not a relic, but a mirror. A piece of the sea born to hold balance, to anchor what I've become.

I place my hand against its chest, just beneath the pulsing light. "Then it's free," I say. "No more cages."

The creature's fins unfurl, rippling outward like sails catching wind. A brilliant pulse radiates from it, racing through the currents, soft but endless. The water shivers with quiet joy.

Thalen drifts closer, the gold thread of his royal current flickering weakly around him. "Its name," he says, almost reverent, "is Lyris."

"Lyris," I repeat, the name fitting like a secret remembered.

The creature—*Lyris*—chirrs softly, voice low and melodic, curling through the water in waves of resonance that feel like laughter.

It swims beside me, its body glowing faintly as it mirrors my movement. The sea feels *alive* and welcoming.

I glance at my father. "You were right about one thing," I say. "The sea does remember its mother."

He looks up, confusion and wonder warring in his gaze.

I smile faintly, running my fingers through the water between Lyris and me. "And now it remembers its child."

The creature sings in answer, and together, we rise through the quiet current—bridge and companion, light and Spark—toward the surface that waits like dawn.

CHAPTER NINETEEN

The Tides

Months have passed since the sea learned to breathe again.

It feels strange to mark time here—where the sun never truly rises, and the water's light is its own—but even the ocean has begun to find rhythm once more. The days flow softly, like the sea has finally settled into its skin. The Pulse hums strong and steady beneath everything now, threading through the currents in waves of gentle blue. Every tide, every shimmer of plankton, every beat of light carries the same truth: *the sea has survived itself.*

I can feel it wherever I swim.

Lurea's coral towers have begun to bloom again, their walls alive with new colors that shift and breathe like the scales of fish. No longer rigid, they move with the current, shaped by it instead of against it. The streets are alive too—filled with laughter, the sound of tailfins cutting through water, and the occasional gleam of sunlight slipping down through the Light Veil above.

Both Flowed and Drain swim the same city currents.

The rebellion ended with collapse. When the throne fractured, the ocean rewrote its rules. The gods' silence didn't bring ruin—it brought freedom. The sea found balance, and in that balance, a new kind of peace.

I move unseen through it all, the current parting softly around me. My reflection flickers faintly in the water—half light, half shadow, no longer quite mortal, no longer bound to the depths. I've become something else, something the priests never named: a watcher, a whisper, a current without crown or altar.

Zeke rules in my place.

Not as king, but as regent—caretaker, not ruler. He wears no coral sigil, no crown, no mantle of gold. Only the light of his own current, bright and sincere. The Council, once full of fear, now looks to him for guidance. He listens—truly listens—in ways our father never could. The priests speak less of obedience now, and more of understanding. They no longer bless with fire or gold, but with coral seeds, pressed into the hands of children as promises of renewal.

And at Zeke's side, the young heirs of both bloodlines train together in the new Guilds. Among them, my sister.

Saphra has grown taller, her movements graceful and deliberate. Her laughter echoes through the halls of the rebuilt palace like light refracted through glass. She studies under the Bloom Guild now—the healers, the growers, the keepers of coral. She tends to the youngest reefs, coaxing them to life with careful hands.

Her touch heals faster than any salve, her voice soothing even to the most fragile coral sprigs.

She will be the heart this sea needs.

I watch her sometimes from afar, my current hidden in the deep shadows beneath the palace gardens. She doesn't know I'm there, but she smiles often, as if she senses something just beyond her sight. She speaks to the coral like she's talking to an old friend. Perhaps, in some way, she is. The ocean remembers, after all.

Thalen—my father—no longer sits a throne. He wanders the southern reefs, far from the city, where the coral meets the sunlit shallows. I've seen him there once or twice, though I never let him see me. He spends his days cataloging fish migrations, mapping new currents, his hands calloused from work rather than rule.

Sometimes, I wonder if he thinks of her—of our mother, the Queen who became the Pulse. Maybe he still listens for her voice in the current. Maybe, like me, he hears her in the soft rhythm of the waves.

The Drains, once exiled to the Hollow, now serve as guardians of the new currentways. They patrol not as soldiers, but as tenders—guides of flow and pressure, ensuring balance between the deep and the surface. Their armor has changed; no longer black and bone-bright, but adorned with living coral that grows and shifts with them.

Even the Flowed have changed. Their golden shields, once symbols of separation, now carry blue streaks along the edges—a quiet acknowledgment that the sea belongs to no single will.

The world below is whole again, and yet I don't belong to it anymore.

I move through it like a dream, a flicker of light glimpsed at the edge of sight. I speak through currents, not words. A gentle surge to calm a storm. A whisper of warmth to guide a lost ship back to safety. A spark of energy to bring the reefs back to bloom when the cold currents threaten.

The Flowed call it the *Tidekeeper's Hand.*
The Drains call it *the Bridge's Whisper*.
But they both mean the same thing: the sea listens now.

And through it, I listen too.

The sea speaks in whispers now, softer than before but full of meaning. Not commands, not cries—just small truths carried by current. The sway of coral gardens stretching open to light, the rhythmic churn of sand over buried relics, the murmur of whales weaving through the deeps like storytellers returning home.

Everywhere I drift, I hear something new. The currents have begun to build their own language again—one of restoration, not fear. The reefs hum like living instruments, their colors deepening with each cycle of flow. The plankton sing faintly under the moonlight, scattering light like stars scattered across the sea's ceiling. Even the great trenches, once dark and silent, now pulse faintly with warmth from the Heartwake's renewed glow.

Above the cities, light filters through in slow motion, breaking into prisms that fall like gentle rain. Children play in the flow, their laughter drifting through the water as they chase darting silverfish and threads of glowing kelp. The Drains and the Flowed swim among one another now, not as rivals but as neighbors, their armor exchanged for simple woven coral bands. Markets bustle again, built into coral arches that sway with the tide.

I drift unseen through them sometimes. The people call the faint currents that brush their hair *the Bridge's blessing,* believing it's a sign of luck, a soft promise from the sea itself. They don't know that it's me—that I guide the smaller pulses, the steady drifts that heal, the soft tides that balance the warmth and cold.

I don't need them to know. Their laughter is enough. Their peace is enough.

In the deep hours, when the sea stills and light fades, I visit the Heartwake. Its glow has softened to something constant and alive, the pulse slow but steady, always reaching outward. I can feel her there—Mother—woven into every rhythm of the current. She doesn't speak anymore, not in words, but I know her voice when it brushes through me. Her love hums through the depths, endless and tender.

Sometimes, I answer. Not with speech, but with Spark—tiny flares of light that echo her pulse, reminders that her daughter still listens.

And the sea listens back.

Above the Heartwake, kelp and coral bloom in impossible colors, blending in ways that never existed before. The ocean is remaking itself—adapting, experimenting, thriving. What was once fracture has become form. The gods are gone, and in their absence, life has learned how to dream again.

I swim through that dream, through the ever-shifting colors and the warmth of rebirth. The current plays with my hair, pulling me gently toward the open sea.

That's when I feel her—before I see her.

A hum through the water, soft and resonant, the same frequency that once met my Spark. The energy wraps around me like the touch of an old friend.

Lyris swims beside me, her glow soft and constant. Her body has grown since we first met, long fins trailing behind like ribbons of silk. She moves with the grace of tide and thunder, quiet but powerful. The connection between us hums as naturally as breath—two currents braided together.

When I touch her side, the Spark answers through her scales, flashing in faint ripples of light. I feel her thoughts, her joy, her endless curiosity. She is the ocean's first child of the new world, born of Spark and sea.

"Where do we go next?" I murmur.

She hums low, her sound vibrating through the water, both question and answer.

The Heartwake pulses faintly behind us. Its glow has softened to a steady rhythm now, no longer volatile, no longer a wound. It beats like a living heart—Selara's heart—still anchoring the world. I can feel her within it, steady and patient, watching.

It's time, her voice whispers through the current. *Go see what waits above.*

I smile.

Lyris moves ahead, fins catching the last tendrils of the Heartwake's light. Together, we rise.

The ascent is long and slow. The deeper currents slide past in soft spirals of color, carrying fragments of life in their flow. Forests of kelp stretch upward like golden towers, swaying in gentle motion. Schools of fish flash silver and violet as we pass, their bodies forming perfect circles before scattering into the light.

We drift through the ruins of old shrines, the once-grand idols now half-swallowed by coral blooms. The carvings of the gods are worn smooth, their faces reclaimed by living reefs. Tiny creatures crawl over them, weaving nests of algae and shell. The sea has forgotten their names, but not their lessons. Even stone returns to life in time.

Further up, the water grows warmer. Sunlight filters through in long, bending shafts, turning everything gold and silver. The closer we get to the surface, the faster the current flows, carrying the scent of salt and air—two worlds blending, breathing together.

I pause once, looking down. The Heartwake glows far below, its light pulsing like a heartbeat across the entire sea. Around it, life moves freely: the Drains tending coral gardens, the Flowed rebuilding their sanctuaries, children swimming between them, laughter threading through the current.

The ocean no longer separates. It *connects*.

Lyris circles me once, her light reflecting in my eyes. I reach out, brushing her side. “Let’s go.”

She surges upward, cutting through the upper bands of current with effortless grace. The Light Veil shimmers above us—a curtain of rippling gold where sea meets sky. I can feel its hum, soft and steady, alive with new equilibrium.

I take one last breath of water, though I no longer need to. The Spark hums in my veins, steady and calm. The current coils around me, then releases.

We break the surface.

Light explodes around us—real light, sunlight—flooding my vision with impossible brightness. The wind hits my face like a forgotten touch, sharp and cool. The sea laps gently against my shoulders, its rhythm syncing with my pulse.

I gasp, not from pain but wonder.

Air fills my lungs. Water flows through them too. For the first time, I breathe both.

Lyris breaches beside me, her body arcing through the sunlit spray before diving again, sending droplets glittering through the air like jewels. The horizon stretches endlessly, the surface a living mirror. Clouds drift above, lazy and white.

The world smells different here—salt and storm, freedom and beginning.

I look upward.

Lightning flickers along the far horizon, bright and clean against the endless blue. A storm is gathering—but not the kind that destroys. This one hums with creation, with the charge of new life.

I close my eyes and let the wind touch my skin. My hair fans out behind me, weightless. The Spark hums softly beneath my ribs, echoing the thunder's call.

Lyris circles me again, and I feel no division between the worlds. The air, the water, the light—they're all the same now, flowing through me as easily as breath.

I smile, the horizon reflected in my eyes.

Below us, the Heartwake pulses once, sending a wave of gold light racing across the sea. The reefs answer, their colors deepening. The creatures rise with it, their bodies shining in the stormlight.

The light ripples outward in a vast ring, sweeping across the ocean like a sunrise beneath the surface. It slides through forests of kelp, igniting them in green fire. It drapes over coral fields, coaxing flowers of light to bloom from their branches. The pulse touches everything—the smallest plankton, the oldest leviathan—and each responds in its own rhythm.

From the abyss, the great shapes stir: translucent giants whose fins shimmer like silk banners, creatures older than memory drawn upward to feel the warmth of a reborn sea. They spiral through the currents in slow, graceful arcs, their movements weaving trails of living light that paint the dark.

Near the shallows, the Flowed look up from their coral cities, eyes wide as the water around them glows in waves of color. Children reach out their hands, and the light clings to their fingers like gold dust. In the Hollow far below, the Drains stand along the ridges of their rebuilt terraces, faces lifted as the warmth of the current sweeps over them. No one speaks; they only *feel*—a single breath shared across the sea.

The pulse reaches the ruins of the old sanctums next, where stone statues of gods have long crumbled to bone-white coral. The light winds through their hollow eyes, filling them, for the first and last time, with life. The carvings dissolve into the flow, surrendering their shape back to the ocean that birthed them.

Every current, every ripple, answers in kind. Schools of fish flash like constellations in motion, swirling upward in great spirals that catch the light and scatter it in ribbons of blue and rose. The water itself vibrates, humming with warmth and color until the entire ocean seems to breathe in time.

High above, the storm breaks open the sky. Lightning veers across the horizon, its reflection cascading through the sea like veins of fire. Each strike answers the Heartwake's glow, forming a bridge of light between sky and water, air and current.

I can feel the shift as it settles—the rhythm that used to flow one way now turning in both directions, circling endlessly. The current loops through me, through Lyris, through every living thing, binding all of us in a single, unbroken tide.

A new current moves beneath the waves, alive and unending—a current that flows both ways.

I tilt my face toward the sky, the Spark thrumming in my chest.

The thunder rolls. The sea responds.

I whisper into the wind, to the sea, to my mother and every god that came before: "Let the tides remember us."

Lightning splits the horizon. Lyris calls out, her voice rising like song. I laugh—truly laugh—for the first time since the sea learned to speak.

A new Age of Tides has begun.

EPILOGUE

FIVE YEARS LATER

The sea has forgotten how to be still.

Five years have passed since the Spark remade the tides, and the ocean still hums with that quiet, living rhythm—endless motion, endless rebirth. The Heartwake no longer burns or trembles; it breathes. Its glow has softened into a golden pulse that lights the trench from below, steady and sure, like the heartbeat of a mother sleeping.

From its warmth, the world has grown new.

Coral forests stretch for miles, their colors deeper than any the old records ever described. They sway with the current, not resisting it but shaping to its rhythm, sheltering creatures that never existed before—the offspring of light and tide, the first of the true hybrid kind. Fins edged in static, eyes like lanterns, veins that shimmer with trace electricity. The sea has evolved to match its own pulse.

Above the Hollow, cities bloom again, though they no longer rise like fortresses. They float. Great coral discs, tethered to the current rather than to the ground, drift slowly through the open water, catching sunlight and scattering it across the deep. The Flowed and Drains live side by side now, their borders dissolved into movement and exchange. The old words—rebellion, exile, purity—sound strange when spoken aloud.

Every moon cycle, the people gather in the shallows beneath the Light Veil. There, the surface glows faintly, where air and water blur together. They release spheres of bioluminescent coral into the current—offerings not to gods, but to the sea itself. They call it the *Festival of Breath*.

At its center stands Zeke.

He never took a crown. He rules by guidance, not decree, and his word carries because it listens. The people call him the Regent of Tides—a title he wears lightly, as though afraid the current might hear it and decide it belongs to someone else. His hair has lightened with the years, his eyes sharp and kind.

At his side is Saphra, the Heir of Bloom. She's grown into her promise—steady, patient, radiant. Her hands glow with soft coral light when she works, coaxing gardens from ruin. The Bloom Guild thrives under her care, and the reefs sing when she passes, their color deepening in gratitude. She's become what our mother once was—the balance between tenderness and power, between creation and restraint.

They speak often of *her*, of the Queen who became the sea. Children in Lurea grow up hearing the story of Selara's heart and the daughter who bridged two worlds. The priests no longer preach of divine wrath;

they teach of harmony, of coexistence, of currents flowing both ways. The sea no longer demands worship—it inspires devotion.

As for me...

I drift through the waters beyond their reach, between the places where light fades and darkness hums. The Spark has changed me more than time ever could. My body no longer feels confined to one shape. Sometimes, I am form—hands, voice, breath. Other times, I am movement—a current brushing through coral, a whisper that guides a lost whale back to her pod, a flicker of light that startles a sleeping reef awake.

I am the sea's wandering pulse now.

Lyris swims beside me still, her fins longer and more translucent than ever, her glow soft as dawnlight. When we pass through the ruins of the old palaces, her hum fills the water—low and melodic, like the echo of memory. The coral there no longer decays. It grows around the wreckage, transforming stone into sanctuary.

We visit the Heartwake each year on the same day. The light greets us as though it remembers. I can feel my mother there still—steady, patient, eternal. She doesn't speak, but her rhythm thrums through the entire sea.

Every so often, I hear Zeke's voice carried through the current, relaying messages meant for me—stories of how the surface has begun to change. The storms are softer now. The air smells cleaner, the sky more vibrant. Birds linger longer near the sea, unafraid of the water's pull. He says the ocean's breath has calmed the world above, too.

Sometimes I wonder what it would feel like to live there—to walk again on the sand I once dreamed of. To breathe only air. To listen to the ocean from afar instead of being it. But the thought fades as quickly as it comes. I am where I belong—between.

The current shifts, and I lift my gaze upward. The Light Veil shimmers faintly above, ribbons of gold bending and flowing in the motion of distant waves. Beyond it, the surface waits, patient as always.

Lyris circles me once, her hum questioning.

"Not today," I tell her, though I can't help but smile.

She chirrs softly and turns, tail sweeping arcs of light through the water. Together, we descend toward the deeper currents, where warmth and color entwine.

As we go, the sea stirs behind us—the same pulse, the same rhythm, the same harmony of Spark and wave.

And though no one can see me now, I know the people of Lurea can *feel* me. The children who touch the water and laugh when it responds. The healers who listen to the current and swear they hear a heartbeat there. The sailors who surface through storms and whisper that the ocean itself guided them home.

They call it luck. They call it mercy.

I call it *listening*.

I look down at my hands, the faint blue glow still alive beneath my skin. It's softer now, steady as a heartbeat. My mother's voice hums within it, carried on every tide.

The sea doesn't end. It transforms.

As the currents shift, as coral and creatures dance in the wake of another dawn, I close my eyes and whisper her words once more—words that have never left me, words the ocean now hums to itself:

Harmony isn't sameness. It's survival.

The Pulse answers, calm and infinite. The tides flow both ways. Somewhere between them—alive, eternal, unbroken—I remain.

Stay Connected

Hey there, amazing reader!

I hope you enjoyed diving into my world of stories as much as I loved creating them! Your thoughts and feedback mean everything to me, and I'd love to hear what you think. Whether it's a review, a favorite quote, or just a quick "OMG, I need more!"—I'm all ears!

Your Reviews Matter! If you loved what you just read (or even if you have thoughts on how it made you feel), leaving a review helps more readers discover my books. Plus, it totally makes my day!

Let's stay connected! Follow me, tag me, and send me a message—I love chatting with fellow book lovers!

Blog: MyuniqueGreen.com
Instagram: @_cmajor_
Snapchat: Cece_major

Can't wait to hear from you! Until next time—keep turning those pages!

About Myunique

Myunique C. Green is a versatile and celebrated author whose work spans across genres, including mystery, thriller, young adult fiction, dystopian science fiction, and personal memoir. Based in Houston, Texas, she began her literary journey with the independently published *Bloodlines: Everything That Glitter* in 2012, which climbed to the Top 10 on Amazon Kindle's Bestseller list. Since then, she has continued to captivate readers with her unique voice and compelling storytelling.

Her titles, such as *713*, a chart-topping mystery short story, and *Grand Rising*, a dystopian epic, showcase her ability to explore complex themes and engage audiences with fresh perspectives. Myunique's deeply personal memoir, *To Mend a Broken Heart*, stands out as a powerful testament to resilience and healing, inspiring readers with her honesty and courage.

Known for her innovative approach and emotional depth, Myunique's writing reflects her passion for tackling challenging narratives that resonate with readers on both an emotional and intellectual level. She has received accolades for her work, including an award from the Midtown Journal for her short fiction.

Excerpt From

Reaping 101

I push open the front door, the familiar scent of home greeting me—something warm and savory simmering on the stove. The clink of pots and pans echoes faintly from the kitchen, where my mom is undoubtedly in the middle of her dinner prep routine. She's always in the kitchen this time of day, usually humming to herself, following recipes as if they're sacred rituals passed down through generations.

"Hey, Mom," I call out as I toss my backpack on the floor by the stairs, feeling the weight finally slide off my shoulders. "What's for dinner?"

"Hey, sweetie!" she replies, her voice light and sing-songy, even though I can hear the clatter of a pan hitting the stove a little harder than usual. "I'm making that chicken casserole you love. It'll be ready soon. How was school?"

"Same as always," I say, walking toward the kitchen for a moment, but then pausing before actually going in. She's too busy for small talk right now, and honestly, I'm too drained to explain the weird vibe of my day. "I'm gonna go soak for a bit. I'll be down when dinner's ready."

“Alright, just don’t fall asleep in there!” she calls after me with a laugh, the one that only half hides her mom-worry about all things bathroom-related.

I roll my eyes affectionately and head upstairs, but not before popping my head into my dad’s office, the door half-cracked open as usual. I give the room a quick glance—his desk is cluttered with paperwork, the computer monitor still glowing, and his chair slightly askew—but no sign of him.

Not surprising.

He’s probably still at work, which seems to be the norm these days. It used to bug me more when I was younger, the way he was always putting in extra hours at the office or bringing work home like it was a second lifeline. Now, I’ve kind of accepted it. He lives for his job, and I guess that’s just how he copes with... whatever it is he’s avoiding.

“Workaholic,” I mutter under my breath as I shut the door quietly. I head up the stairs, feeling my legs grow heavier with each step, the day’s exhaustion settling deep into my bones.

By the time I reach my room, the idea of soaking in a hot bath feels like the only good decision I’ve made today. I head straight for the bathroom, twisting the knobs and letting the water flow, steam rising up in thick, comforting waves. A deep breath in, a long exhale out. Bubbles and bath salts, the calming kind that smell like lavender or eucalyptus—whatever this stuff is—it’ll do the trick. I pour a generous amount into the water and watch as it fizzes and foams up, filling the tub with soft, pearly bubbles.

The moment I sink in, the heat wraps around me like a cocoon, and I can practically feel the tension melt out of my muscles. I lean my head back against the cool tile and close my eyes, letting myself drift for a moment. My mind wanders, like it always does in moments like this.

I think about Katie and Jess, how easy things seem for them, even when they're not. I think about Matthew—because of course, I do. And then I think about that strange, creeping feeling I had earlier in the car, that fleeting moment of dread that didn't quite make sense.

But now, in the warmth of the bath, it feels far away. Almost like I imagined it. Maybe I'm just tired, maybe my brain's been playing tricks on me. It happens.

As I lie there, the bubbles rising higher around me, I start to feel more relaxed. My breathing slows, my heartbeat steady. The bathroom is quiet, save for the faint drip of the faucet and the groan of the house settling around me. I sink a little deeper into the water, letting it cover my shoulders, soaking away the remnants of the day. Dinner should be ready soon, I think, and I'll feel better after eating. Just a few more minutes of—

A sudden, cold rush of air sweeps over me, cutting through the steam like a blade. It's so sharp, so out of place, that my eyes snap open in an instant.

There it is again—that chilling sensation. It starts in my chest, like before, but this time it spreads, crawling up my spine and down to my fingertips. My breath catches, and for a second, I'm not sure if I should move or stay perfectly still.

The bathroom is the same as it was a moment ago—nothing has changed. The water is still hot, the bubbles still surrounding me, but the air... the air feels wrong.

My pulse quickens, and I sit up a little in the tub, glancing around, trying to figure out why my body is suddenly on high alert. It's as if the room itself is colder, but that doesn't make sense. My skin prickles, and I pull my knees to my chest, wrapping my arms around them as though it'll shield me from whatever invisible thing just passed through.

I sit there, listening.

Nothing. No footsteps, no movement, just the soft gurgle of the water lapping against the tub.

I try to shake it off again—convince myself it's all in my head—but the chill doesn't leave this time. It lingers, pressing down on me with this strange heaviness that makes my skin crawl.

This is different from earlier, I realize. Stronger. More... present.

"Get a grip, Chloe," I mutter to myself, forcing a weak laugh to slice through the stress.

But the feeling remains, gnawing at the pit of my stomach. Something's wrong.

The feeling lingers, heavy and insistent. No matter how much I try to shove it aside, it keeps seeping back in, wrapping itself around my chest like a tightening rope. My mind is racing now, darting between half-formed thoughts, none of them making sense. Why do I feel like this? What is this?

I try to relax, sinking back into the water, but it doesn't help. The warmth that had been so comforting a moment ago now feels stifling, like I'm being held under, trapped. My breath quickens, and the weight in the room presses down harder.

I can't take it anymore.

If it won't leave, then I will.

In a rush, I stand up, water sloshing over the sides of the tub, bubbles sliding down my arms and legs. The cool air hits my skin, but instead of relief, I feel exposed—vulnerable in a way I can't explain. I reach for the edge of the tub, ready to step out, to escape this creeping sensation.

But my foot catches on the slick porcelain, and before I can even register what's happening, my balance gives way.

I slip.

The world tilts, and my head smashes into the side of the tub with a sharp, nauseating crack.

For a split second, everything goes dark. The water splashes around me, my body half-submerged and sprawled awkwardly on the cold tile floor.

Then the dread is gone.

Just like that, the heavy, suffocating feeling that had been gnawing at me vanishes, leaving in its place a strange, hollow confusion. My ears ring, and there's a tingling sensation at the base of my neck, spreading outward, like tiny needles prickling just beneath my skin.

I lie there for a moment, dazed, trying to catch my breath. What the heck just happened?

The pain throbs in my skull, but not as bad as I'd expect. It's more the shock than anything—the suddenness of it. My limbs feel heavy, awkward, and for a second, I think about just staying down here, waiting for whatever weirdness was happening to pass. But I can't. I won't.

I sit up slowly, feeling the room swirl for a moment before steadying. The tiles beneath me are cold, and water drips from my body in fat droplets, puddling around me. I glance back at the tub, half-expecting to see something there—some reason for this whole bizarre episode. But it's just a tub. Just water. Just bubbles.

With a shaky breath, I pull myself up, leaning against the wall for support. My head throbs, but I can move, so it's not that bad. I grab my towel and wrap it around myself, the soft fabric warm against my cold, wet skin. The confusion lingers, but the dread is gone. And, honestly, that's good enough for me right now.

I head for my bedroom, trying to brush off the last remnants of whatever just happened. Dinner will be ready soon, and I just want to put on some comfy clothes and pretend this day hasn't been one weird moment after another.

But before I can even get dressed, a scream rips through the house.

A gut-wrenching, animalistic scream that freezes me in my tracks.

My mom.

It's coming from the bathroom. The same one I just left.

Every hair on my body stands on end. My pulse spikes as I rush to the door, heart pounding in my ears. Panic claws at my throat. My hand reaches for the doorknob, but when I try to turn it, it won't budge.

I twist it harder.

Nothing.

It's stuck.

"No, no, no!" I mutter under my breath, yanking at the knob again, my heart racing faster with every second.

Another scream—this one even more guttural, more filled with terror than before—tears through the air, and I feel my blood turn to ice.

Something is wrong. Something is very, very wrong.

The door still won't budge, no matter how hard I twist the knob. My hands are shaking now, my breath coming out in shallow gasps. Another scream cuts through the air, and this one is worse—ragged and desperate, like something deep inside is breaking.

I take a step back, my mind spinning, my heart in my throat. The cold creeps in again, chilling me to my core. But this time, it's different. It's not just a feeling. The temperature in the room *actually* drops. The air gets heavy, like the whole atmosphere is waiting for something—something I don't want to meet.

I swallow hard, forcing myself to calm down. It's just a panic attack. That's what this is. Right? Except when I blink, someone's there. Standing casually in the corner of my room like they belong there. A guy.

But not just any guy.

He's dressed in a worn-out hoodie, faded jeans, and sneakers, like he just stepped out of a college campus instead of... wherever Death is supposed to come from. He's tall, with a kind of lanky build, dark hair falling messily over his forehead. He looks... tired. Not just tired—*exhausted.* Like the world has been weighing him down for centuries. Which, apparently, it has.

He lets out a long, irritated sigh, pulling his hood back. "Great. Just great," he mutters, rubbing his eyes like this whole thing is a massive inconvenience.

I stare at him, my mouth open, trying to reconcile this normal-looking, disgruntled guy with the fact that I can't seem to move or speak or *breathe* properly.

He catches my eye and gives me a once-over, then groans. "Ah, man. I *really* didn't want to do this today."

"What... what are you...?" I manage to stammer out, my brain trying to catch up with what's happening. Because this? This is not normal. Nothing about this moment is normal.

The guy rolls his eyes and takes a step forward, hands stuffed in his hoodie pockets. "Who do you think I am, kid? Santa Claus? No. I'm Death." He says it like it's the most obvious thing in the world. "I know, I know. Not what you were expecting, right? Everyone's always waiting for the big black robe and scythe bit. So cliché. It's 2024. We're past that."

I blink, utterly dumbfounded. "You're Death?"

He spreads his arms, as if saying, *ta-da!* "Yep. The one and only. Been collecting souls for millennia. And let me tell you"—he gives me a pointed look—"I'm tired. Seriously, I need a break."

My brain is doing somersaults. I'm standing here in a towel, still dripping from the bath, and *Death* is casually chatting with me like he's some guy who got lost on his way to Starbucks.

He sighs again, the weariness in his expression growing as he glances at the bathroom door. "Look, I'm not trying to drag this out. I've got, like, a hundred souls to collect before midnight, so let's just—"

"Wait!" I blurt out, panic surging through me. "I—uh, I mean, can't we... I don't know... *talk* about this? I'm not even dead yet! Shouldn't there be, like, a process? Paperwork? Something?"

He gives me a look like I've just asked the stupidest question in the universe. "Do I look like I have time for paperwork? Do you have any idea how many people die every day? It's exhausting."

I stare at him, my mind racing. Okay, so he's Death. That's established. And he's clearly not in a great mood. But he's also... human? Kind of. Maybe I can reason with him.

"Look," I start, trying to keep my voice steady, "what if... what if we make a deal? You're tired, right? You want a break? Maybe you could, like, not take my soul today. Just take a breather. It's been a long day for both of us, and... I'm sure you don't *need* my soul right now, right?"

Death narrows his eyes at me, clearly skeptical. "You're trying to weasel your way out of this, huh? You're not the first to try, kid."

I force a shrug, though my heart is hammering in my chest. "Maybe. But I mean, if you're that tired... what's one more day, right?"

He rubs his temples like he's fighting off a headache. "Why do people always think they're special?" he mutters to himself before looking back at me. "Fine. You've got, like, ten minutes to convince me. But if you waste my time, I'm dragging you over to the other side so fast your head will spin. Got it?"

"Got it," I say, swallowing the lump in my throat.

Okay. Ten minutes to convince Death not to kill me. No pressure.

www.ingramcontent.com/pod-product-compliance
Lightning Source LLC
LaVergne TN
LVHW020713110826
845149LV00012B/2252

* 9 7 8 1 1 0 5 8 9 6 0 5 7 *